SIMPLE ARITHMETIC

A Chiaroscuro Tale for Adults

by

S. E. REDMOND

DEDICATION

To Jerrid

CONTENTS

ACKNOWLEDGMENTS

Allan Fawcett   for the cover illustration

Rune Vibegaard and Inga Sigurjonsdottir   for a first reading

Beth Dickson   for technical help and friendship

Marlene Siering   for perceptive comments

CHAPTER ONE

Why Victor and Brenda met in Florence, Italy to discuss a problem in Iowa is a mystery. Yet it seems a suitable place for a quarrel, since the city in its various reincarnations over centuries was often an unforgiving place, and Victor and Brenda arrived that January in no mood to forgive each other, or anybody else. They were not bad people, or even quarrelsome, only both were by then on a teeter-totter of moral choice – on their way down, in their different ways,

Memory is a tricky and mysterious mistress. We need objects to remind us that we're in thrall to time. Somewhere along the winding road of life - a life with no turning their grandfather had once warned them -Victor and Brenda, estranged brother and sister, each sought a reminder of what had happened to them in Florence. Victor wanted to remember the merry-go-round; Brenda couldn't forget the angel she'd seen on the wall of a Florence hotel breakfast room.

Victor, a man who travelled light throughout his life, came to nurture the tiny detailed merry-go round he bought in a Florence shop dedicated to Tuscan folk art. He kept it beside his bed in whatever room or apartment he rented over the years and may die holding it. The merry-go-round had called forth both bad and good in him. Brenda bought a poster depicting a yellow haired angel, dressed in pink, by a 15th century Tuscan artist. She'd seen the original painting in the Uffizi museum and bought the poster in New York City. It was a large, solid angel with a forefinger raised in warning; she learned, as years went by, what that warning was.

One of the oddities of their January visit to Florence was the mist of opaque air that lingered every morning in the piazza with the merry-go-round. Carlos, who ran and repaired the elderly carousel during the winter - and kept some bottles there he didn't want his wife to know about - saw the mist as he walked to and fro, but didn't think it important. Neither did Estelle, his wife, who ran the cafe nearby. Her attention was devoted to her husband and her customers. She paid no attention to the solitary tourist wandering around on a cold January morning.

In those first mornings in Florence in that piazza, Victor enjoyed himself. He watched the small children sitting in a row on a bench, squirming and giggling as they waited for the merry-go-round to start - a wheel that spun round and round, made hollow mocking music, flashed sudden sharp lights, forced gaudy festooned horses to rise and fall. He noted the smudge of cloud but judged it early morning mist. The three teachers at the A.B.C. nursery school, who took their children to the merry-go-round twice a week, were singing songs to them as they waited for the ride to open. At first they didn't notice the thin, badly dressed tourist standing so close to the giggling children.

Just arrived in Florence, Victor has found work as a free lance tour guide. He's telling himself to be positive. But it's early morning in a city he hasn't seen for two years; he's cold and alone, and afraid. Victor has a little grab bag of fears; they sometimes erupt at unexpected moments. This morning he's afraid of what he's planning to do. That's a new fear. He's also afraid of the Berlin police, who could trace him to Florence – not that he's done real wrong (he tells himself), but has been drifting with a wrong crowd, the drugs at first a mild diversion, a way of socializing, which led him to notice how his acquaintances were paying for their drugs. An old fear is of going back to the U.S., to Iowa, to Cedar Rapids, and to the house and people he grew up with. They know his story, can pick him apart as they did when he was young. His mother and father are dead. Only his sister Brenda still makes a claim on him. She sends Christmas and birthday cards, but he hasn't seen her in ten years. She's threatened to visit him in Italy. Most of all, Victor is afraid of dying poor and alone in Europe.

When Brenda wrote that their mother was dead, enclosing a letter from their mother's lawyer, he knew he had to make a claim for half the family house. If he and Brenda sell it, they will split the money. It's a big old house, a mansion. Their father's father built it during a long spell of money making in the 1920's. That money will keep Victor in Europe for years. All he has to do is sweet talk his sister into selling the house. That won't be easy since he's ignored her for years.

CHAPTER TWO

Her first morning in Florence, Brenda lay spread-eagled across the hotel bed. She hasn't figured out how to turn on the air conditioning and the room is stuffy and over warm, though outside the wind is cold. Still she's happy to be once again in her favorite position – flat on her back in bed. Brenda thinks best that way. So much is happening in her life.

So here I am in Florence. I took a taxi; that's costing me money. I didn't buy a new suitcase; I had the old plaid one of Mama's and the taxi driver, a small, dark -haired man turned up his sharp nose at it. You fat woman and a fat ugly suitcase in my cab? I could hear him thinking that but I didn't care. I'm in Florence. I booked into the Black and White Hotel not far from the airport. The hotel is bare - French stylish I think- but the elevator is so small and old it seemed to groan as it rose to the third floor. The bed is king sized though and I slept great this afternoon. Now I'll call Victor.

No answer.

She put down the phone, flopped back on the bed.

I'm like a little orphan girl now. Only, drat it I'm not little and Mama's lawyer warned me that we're both named in mama's will; we own the house jointly and anytime soon, I might have to sell it and give half the money to Victor. He refused to come home to Mama's funeral and I haven't forgiven him for that.

If you met Brenda you would find her pleasant and accommodating, never critical, nor abusive, though forthright in expressing her opinions, and occasionally obtrusive in her attempts at organizing others. You might even think she has a small girl inside her, like a pearl in a big oyster, but you would be wrong. Brenda has a strong and angry stranger inside her, someone she's trying to feed and keep away from, like avoiding sleeping with a bear, or living life with a badger. Avoidance, yes but why? Her mother? A kind, simple person - everybody thought - but subjected to a fair amount of abuse over the years, she'd dwindled into a skinny, wretched old crone, 97 pounds of crabby questions. She'd pounced on her daughter whenever possible, especially when Brenda was walking out the door or coming into the house. Why? Where? Who? When? How? Did you? Didn't you? They came rapid fire, the kind of questions that attracted complicated answers, unless you were on your knees salaaming apologies. Brenda discovered it was much, much easier to stay in bed as long as possible. Her room had been on the third floor and her mother rarely wheezed her way up that far.

Brenda doesn't want to sell the house. Now that her demanding mother is dead, she's enjoyed the luxury of lying around doing nothing, going nowhere, She's grown fatter and fatter, more and more comfortable watching television, reading books, planning her food menus. Groceries are delivered; cosmetics, candy, and medication arrive by taxi. She's big, and fat, but solid and well proportioned despite her weight. She has a beautiful round face, with lovely brown eyes. Her hair is ill kept, and flyway so she keeps it short. Her hands and feet are small and plump; she takes care of her nails, but doesn't wear polish. Since her mother's scales broke, she hasn't weighed herself. Lying in comfort on the king sized Black and White Hotel bed, she dialed her brother again; this time Victor answered. He's surprised.

"I don't believe you."

"I said I was booked on Lufthansa; I gave you the date."

"No way you're in Florence; you're pulling my leg."

"I'm here."

5

"Where?"

"At a hotel. Victor, you need to come get me."

"I don't have a car."

Much against her will, Brenda sat up. Push back, like her mama said. "Shall I take a taxi? I don't have a lot of Euros."

"You wait there. Stay at the hotel until I call you. I've got a schedule I have to follow."

He took down her hotel room number.

"What kind of schedule, Victor? What do you do?"

"I'll explain later. Right now I'm busy."

"Doing what?"

"I'm making a video."

She wanted to talk and talk to him because she hadn't talked to anyone who knew her for a long time but Victor hung up.

Soon Brenda was in trouble: The hotel restaurant was closed. There was nowhere nearby to walk to except a dismal little coffee bar. She was hungry, but she couldn't find much there; she bought a bottle of water and some buns and a pudding and took them back to the room, but they were strangers; they didn't know her. She laid them out on the bed, like they were friends, but it didn't work. She talked instead to her friend, Jesus, and Jesus said, never mind, eat everything up and go to sleep; tomorrow is another day. Jesus sounds like Mama sometimes, she thought, an awful lot like Mama. I wonder where she is.

The next day she waited and waited, but Victor didn't call; she had nothing to eat. She grew afraid and asked the manager to call her a cab. He did that and also suggested a good restaurant near a Cathedral. She couldn't pronounce the Italian but the taxi driver took her there and it was wonderful – full of people, Italians, all coming and going, eating with each other, but talking, talking, talking; the owner was pretty fat but ran around, and every once and awhile he burst into song, like an opera singer.

Brenda saw that he was happy that they were all eating food in his restaurant. She ordered a steak because it seemed simple; it came with lemon slices on it. She had salad in a big bowl, and she ate and ate, listening to people talking in Italian and she knew they weren't talking about her or judging her; they were talking to each other about their worlds, and the food. She listened to the owner singing an aria of joy over the hum of conversation while she ate a somewhat rare steak, something she'd never eat at home, but the lemon made it taste all right, and she felt like she belonged, that Jesus was helping her to become a better person.

She whispered, "Thank you, Jesus, this is just right."

When the energetic little girl waitress took away her plate, Brenda ordered coffee and sat smiling, loving everything and everyone, and then the owner came over and touched her hair and said something kind and loving. It's Jesus bringing us together, Brenda thought. I don't know whether he's talking about me, or the steak but that doesn't seem to matter.

Of course when she staggered out the door after drinking her coffee and paying the bill with her credit card, she found herself in a narrow cobblestone street. She didn't know where she was or how to speak Italian. It turned out "taxi" is a universal word so when she said it to people they told her to go to the piazza where the taxis waited, and she did. Soon she was at Victor's door, a big wooden door on a cobblestone street. She was frightened, but happy, and only hoped he was there. She rang the bell.

CHAPTER THREE

Victor was back from a successful afternoon with a group of older Americans; he was smiling when he took out his key to open the heavy wooden front door. They'd liked the bit about Renaissance artists using mummy powders, or what they thought were mummy powders, in their paint pigments, because the artists believed ancient embalming would keep their paintings from cracking. He stopped smiling when he turned around to see Brenda drinking coffee at the café across the road. She spotted him and rushed over. The apartment was on Via Ricasoli, a street that boasted several cafes as well as shops. She was pleased with her success; she'd managed to find some boots to fit and at once informed the neighborhood.

"You have to wear boots here," she gushed to her brother who winced at her wide-eyed goggle stare. "The ground is full of stones."

"That's the way the Romans made streets."

"Romans?"

He turned around, unlocked his front door, pushed it slightly open, saw and felt the dark cool air of the hallway. It might be possible to escape.

"This city began as a Roman retirement camp for military officers and soldiers."

Turning around to face his sister, Victor saw for the first time how fat she was. I can't believe it, he thought. Brenda held up her skirt to show off her new boots. He glanced up and down the street, but it was empty except for an occasional scooter scattering raw in-your-face noise.

"I found these boots just up the street; my legs are so fat I couldn't wear most of them but these are lace up. Aren't they pretty?"

He found himself looking, almost against his will. The boots were stylish, a rich almond brown. She has small feet, he thought, how does she carry all that weight around?"

"I think I'm losing weight," Brenda said loudly, "Can I eat supper with you?"

"I haven't much." Again he looked out at the street.

"I'm not that hungry. I had a wonderful lunch. There was a lot of singing. I'm going to do more shopping. I'll come back here."

"No, I'm sorry, Brenda. I have to work this evening. Let's try for tomorrow."

"You're working at home?"

"Yes. And I have impatient clients." He added that with an inner wince. The man in Berlin threatened to send the police after him if a video didn't arrive within a week. Victor had trouble believing that, but still – the client was not a nice man.

"What do you do?" She moved closer; they were face to face. She thought then, with surprise, how blue his eyes were. And how thin his face was.

"Never mind. I said I'd call you when I'm free." His voice crackled with irritation.

"I'm staying at a hotel near the airport. But there's nothing there. It's hard to find something to eat. Victor, can you lend me some Italian money for a taxi? I'm afraid to give them my credit card."

He edged two steps backward, was inside, the comfort of the dim cool hallway embracing him. There was always that smell of floor polish he liked. He pushed the door between them, but Brenda leaned in to speak to him through the narrow crack."I have a letter for you from the lawyer."

"How long are you staying in Florence?"

She pushed the door wider, created a smile that made Victor hate her. "That depends."

"I'll book you a hotel room by the river; you won't have to take taxis."

Brenda moved inside - 'push back, push back" – she could almost hear her mama's voice. "Victor can you give me enough money for two taxi rides? And will you telephone me the name of the hotel you find for me? Will it be close to you?"

He tried to close the door against her again, but she poked a finger through the narrow opening and touched his nose. "Hey, glad to see you brother; it's been a long time."

Leaping backwards, he fumbled in his leather side pouch, pulled out enough Euros to fly her to Rome. "Here. Take this. Did you come through Rome? Are you flying back that way?"

"Frankfurt. It's an awful airport, Victor. Long hallways

and you have to run to catch your plane and nobody helps…"

SLAM.

Victor was gone.

Shocked Brenda stood for a moment in front of the locked door. She knew it was locked because she'd tried it earlier. Walking back across to the café, she stocked up on water, a half bottle of wine, buns, butter, anything she could find that would feed her that evening. She asked about pizza and was directed to another café down the street. As she ate a small pizza, she thought about how strange it was that she'd forgotten the color of Victor's eyes, and that now she was taller than her older brother. She ate, as she usually did, slowly and carefully; the pizza lacked cheese and had something greenish on it she'd never heard of, but it tasted all right. Then she uttered the magic word 'taxi'.

Back at the Black and White Hotel. Brenda lay spread-eagled once more on the wide king-sized bed. She left her almond brown Florence boots on so she could admire them. But she avoided thinking about Victor because the strange way he was behaving makes her feel bad. Since she doesn't like feeling bad, she spread out all the food she'd brought home with her and looked at it while she thought about herself. She did that a lot.

Take time to tell Jesus. I did that today; I'm learning how to control my life. After Charles took himself out the door saying, 'You ain't no woman if you can't take on all of me.' I had to. Course he weighed more than 200 pounds and was six foot five. That was a lot to take on when you have no mother, no brother to help guide you."
Jesus talked to me then. Or maybe I talked to him first. I was alone in the house. Victor gone to Europe, Mama gone to heaven, Charles back with his wife. I talked to Jesus every day.

I guess that's praying. There's way you're supposed to approach God, hailing him/her, thanking him/her, then only then asking for something. But I was lonely so I just asked him questions like: What should I buy at the grocery store, Jesus? And into my head came the words: Good food, buy good food. That's an answer, so I stopped buying all the sweet stuff Mama liked and bought meat and potatoes and pasta and vegetables. But I didn't lose any weight. I kept gaining. When Charles stopped driving me around, I bought a big black truck. Got my hair styled. Went for a manicure every two weeks. Started feeling like a person. Decided being fat wasn't so bad. Met some other fat women and we had some good laughs. But they turned catty on me after awhile, especially when they found out about Charles. So I settled down to eating alone. I like eating. It's like a visit with friends, reliable friends, the kind that won't walk away, or say bitter things.

Thinking this, tears came to her eyes. Her monologues always did that to her. Victor isn't being friendly at all and I've come all this way to negotiate with him in a friendly way like the lawyer suggested.

While Brenda was reviewing her life, Victor found he was too upset to work with the photographs he'd taken from Berlin. Instead he was drinking red wine and thinking about how maybe he could kill Brenda. That would be the best way to end this money problem. Red wine made him think tough.

I don't like that lawyer. A gnome of an elderly man I met at Grand Daddy's funeral. The lawyer - old what's his name– was openly contemptuous of homosexuals. Victor hadn't looked at either the letter or the emails from the man because he'd been so deeply offended by him. He should have known why I went so far away. And I didn't like the proprietary arms of that disgusting man around Mama and Brenda.

Victor's memories of his past life in Cedar Rapids are crystal glass sharp. He's forgotten nothing about growing up there - in that city, that house, in that family. His eyes moistened. I never knew a real sense of self until I got out of there. In Europe, they value a man with an education.

He put away the bottle of red wine, outlined a new guide lecture on points of interest in Florence. Tourists liked his lectures. But January wasn't a busy time. He stood up, stretched, walked around the apartment. I might have to wave my face at more hotels, more tourist agencies. I have to pay the rent. The children waiting for the merry go-round – I could slip one of them away for half an hour - I won't hurt any of them, Victor has always told himself that - it's just that I need the money.

The last few years Victor has been moving around his favorite places: London, Berlin, Florence, but as he grows older it's more difficult to find someone who will pay. He's not a scholar, only someone with a lifelong interest in the arts; wherever he goes he presents himself as capable of guiding tourists around famous statuary and museums. He's been in Berlin, and now has to switch from the decadent 1930's in Germany to the quarrelsome Renaissance in Italy. His under the table business – pornography videos - he keeps secret. German friends took him to Thailand where he discovered how many men were interested in children. He is not, but hopes to find clients in Italy – all those priests he thinks –surely a few monsignors, even cardinals. who might be interested.

The next morning as he worked editing the video he will send back to Germany, he thinks about the visit he and Barry made to a priest's house in northern France. Barry had enticed him into a passionate affair in Paris; neither of them had much money, and so had hitchhiked everywhere. Victor kept his return ticket to London and a few pounds hidden from his new lover, since he discovered Barry operated much more energetically when he thought they had no money. And so it was Barry who rang the bell of the priest's large house in a small town in Brittany.

Victor wrapped up the video for mailing, still thinking about that day standing in the priest's kitchen, which was quite grand and immaculately clean with a large lovely glass bowl full of grapes. Barry had some story about why they had to get to the next town. The priest and he conversed in French so Victor only gathered bits and pieces. Finally the priest disappeared for a few minutes and came back with a rope. Victor remembers how surprised he was – why a rope? Is Barry threatening to hang himself? He seemed awfully dramatic sometimes. The other two men spoke in French, then the priest left the kitchen again. Victor stood in silence; Barry sat down in a chair against the wall. He looked completely at home. He was a tall plump man of forty with expressive hands. He'd folded them as he calmly waited for the priest to return.

Victor remembers how restless and hungry he himself had been, how he'd approached the bowl of fruit suddenly ravenous. Had we eaten that day? he asks himself. Not much more than coffee and croissants. We'd walked ten, twelve hours that day. It was summer, hot - I wanted those grapes, and so walked over to the bowl and started shoving them into my mouth. Barry leapt up, rushed over, grabbed them from my hand. He threw them back into the bowl. A rare sternness was in his face, his voice. "Non. Ne manges pas rien, Rien du tout." he muttered, just as the priest re-entered the room, carrying a rope even stouter than the first .

Soon all three retired to the priest's garage where they were invited into the back seat of a BMW. The priest, a slight, serious-looking Breton wearing black rimmed glasses, drove them at a sedate pace into the next town, and set them down, with the rope, in a parking lot. Barry handed the rope to me, and

I was confused; I didn't know what the rope was for. When the priest said goodbye, Barry became effusive in gratitude; his eyes filled with tears when the priest pressed one hundred and fifty francs into his hand; Barry's voice trembled as he thanked him. The priest started his car.

"What's the rope for?" Victor remembers demanding in a too loud voice. Barry frowned and shook his head. Waving a benediction with one hand, the priest, a thin smile on his face, had driven away.

"Don't ask," Barry had said. He'd leaned over and laughed, laughed until Victor found out the truth. Barry had created a imaginary car stuck in a farmer's field, and a farmer waiting with a tractor to pull the car out of a muddy ditch once a rope was found. Victor could smile then too because everyone was satisfied: The priest had done a good deed; Barry got what he wanted, and they could sell the rope and have money to spend.

I was happy that day, Victor thought with some surprise; we bought ourselves good wine and a hot supper with the priest's money. Plus I learned something– we weren't beggars. We would never be beggars. I have to remember that. Without resources, but unlike gypsies who snatch and run, they'd presented themselves as simple wayfarers with a transportation problem. Barry had introduced them appropriately. And Victor had learned that priests would help strangers when asked. Now he was finding his own way to survive, a way to present himself. But still he moved around his small apartment with a little tremor of distress. Life alone was no fun; doing what he was doing was no fun.

Downstairs, he opened the big scarred door right into Brenda. Oh my god.

She clutched his arm. "Guess what happened to me?"

"I'm busy."

"I have to talk to you. I have to tell you what happened to me last night. Do you know what happened to me last night? A man followed me."

Victor lifted her clutching hand off his shoulder, squeezed himself past her - she was blocking the door –and once outside managed to reach around her and grab the doorknob, ready to close the door.

"Got to go sweetheart."

"An awful man followed me all the way to the hotel. Don't you want to know?"

"No. Get out of the way."

"Don't you care?"

"Not at this moment." He demonstrated his white teeth without the least hint of a smile. "Please move. I have to mail a package. And I have a tour this afternoon."

She moved out into the street, watched her brother shut his door with an emphatic yank. He walked away, not fast, not slow, but not looking back. She followed him,

"I'll go with you. I get lost sometimes."

They walked single file, Brenda trailed behind him. He pretended she wasn't there; He turned right, turned left; they were beside the Duomo Cathedral.

"It's a big church isn't it? Have you been inside? What's it like inside?"

She was puffing a little. Stopping to look in windows, she saw leather jackets, purses, boots, found one shop full of leather; out of it drifted a delicious odor, of brown leather, red leather, blue leather, green leather, all the colors with the same smell of satisfaction, luxury, plentitude. A tall thin girl, dressed in a big collared, brown wool sweater, emerged in the doorway of the leather world. "Want to step inside? Find something you like?"

"I like it all," Brenda said, "I like the smell."

The girl didn't smile. "Yes?"

She's doesn't like me, Brenda thought, one of those nibbling little thoughts that made her hands prickle. She shook her head and moved away, looking ahead to see where Victor was, only he wasn't there – not here, not there, not anywhere.

When she was a child, trying to follow him to school, she used to think he looked for secret ways to get there so nobody saw him. But usually, she figured out how to track him down. As a child, it seemed like that was her job, not to let Victor get out of sight. But that day she was soon tired and hungry, and went back to the hotel by taxi, stopping only for a coffee and a treat, and to buy some supper.

Victor chortled when he saw he'd lost her. He didn't believe his sister's story about being followed. She used to tell the most astounded lies when she was a little girl. But there were only three tourists waiting at the agency, and his walking tour of writers' houses was cancelled. He walked around until it started to rain, then went home, ate a bowl of canned soup, went to bed, somehow more unhappy than usual.

CHAPTER FOUR

In her old hotel room by the airport, Brenda ate all the food she'd laid out on the bed, food she'd bought in town. The room was cold; she missed the comforter and many pillows she had at home. She ate the ham and cheese sandwiches, the two oranges, drank the little bottle of rose wine. Some of the little plastic cartons had strange food in them and she threw them away.

I should have brought murder mysteries to read. My favorite time's at night in bed, with a box of chocolates and a murder mystery. Mama didn't approve of mysteries for nice girls. And Daddy thought chocolates had caffeine in them and made women too emotional. Chocolates weren't allowed in the house.

After her mama died, Brenda spent slow careful times, reading the little diagrams of choices in the chocolate boxes she bought, laying out three new mystery books to choose from on the bedside table. Sometimes she'd stayed up all night.

What to do tonight? What are my choices? As she tore the wrapping off a chocolate bar from the vending machine in the hotel basement, she thought of her daddy. He never understood that choices are important. He hated people being emotional - his anger was more than emotion, it was some kind of brain attack. He threw chairs around. Once he threw the dog through the window. And he was mean to Victor. And Mama. I never saw Mama cry. I don't cry. I don't know what it feels like. I think I cried when Mama died, but only a little. I hardly remember those weeks when I found her dead in the pantry;

I guess I should have made her a sandwich.

How can I sell the house? That's not my choice –to sell the house. The house is my safety. I have to explain that to Victor. I've tried to but he gets angry. On the phone, he said he'd come home, hire his own lawyer, and force me to sell. But then he gave me his address in Florence so I came. But now he doesn't want me here at all. Not to talk to that's for sure. She unwrapped another chocolate bar. He's awfully thin. He probably doesn't eat enough. He never used to eat at home when we were children.

The next day, at noon, Brenda arrived at the apartment. When Victor answered the doorbell, there she was, smile on her face, and a pizza in her hands. "I brought lunch,"

He stepped back, tried to block her but she pushed past him. "I came to visit. I don't have a key. You should give me a key. Are you working?"

"No."

She lumbered over to touch the tall metal gate standing between the foyer and the stairs.

"That's funny. Is it locked?"

"Not during the day."

Then they were up the stairs. After three flights, she was panting. "Don't they have an elevator?"

"Did you see one?"

She flopped on the couch in the living room and looked around, "This is nice."

"I lucked out. Living room, kitchen, bathroom, two bedrooms. Not bad for Florence."

"You have another bedroom?"

"That's my workroom."

"What are you doing in there?"

"I'll find you a hotel - if you must stay."

"We have to talk."

"Yes. I own half the house."

He stood by the door, moved to stand in front of the window. Outside, the narrow sidewalks were full of pedestrians conducting conversations single file.

"The title hasn't been changed. It's still in Mama's name." said Brenda. She sat slumped on the shabby black leather sofa; Victor, arms folded, sat down beside her. Touched her.

"I'll find you a hotel near the airport."

She pulled away. "No. The one I'm in is too far out. And it's horrid. The men around there -I told you I was followed. One old man cursed me. He called me names."

Victor moved. " Let's eat. Bring your pizza into the kitchen. What kind is it?"

"I don't know. I just pointed.' At the kitchen table, he made the mistake of sitting directly across from her. He couldn't take his eyes off his sister as she ate her way through two pieces of pizza. She's chewing with her mouth open. And how did she get so fat? She wasn't fat when I left. Chubby maybe but she was only fourteen. He reached over took a single piece of pizza. Using a knife and fork he ate it slowly, delicately. Then took another piece, ate it slowly too. Then another.

"A deluxe, I think," he said. "Do you want some wine? Or water? I don't have much else. I don't drink pop, you must remember that - even when I was a kid."

He rose, collected a half empty bottle of red wine, set it on the table, then reached behind to take two glasses from the drainer. She leaned back and smiled, nodded her head.

"Good pizza. Next time I'll bring some beer. We should eat lunch together every day."

Suppressing a shudder, he poured two glasses, than sprang up, picked up his cell phone, and walking away into the other room, talked into it, then called from that distance, "How long are you staying, Brenda?"

"I don't know."

"I have no money to pay your bills."

"I brought my credit card."

Victor was walking in circles in the living room. She ate another piece of pizza. He walked back into the kitchen.

"Four days," Victor said into his cell phone and shut it off. "You have a hotel room near the river, Brenda. For four days."

"What river?"

"The Arno. You can walk along the paths. It's a bit far from here, but you'll like it."

He sat down opposite her. They looked at each other, sat in silence studying each other, she smiling, he scowling. She leaned forward so that her chin almost touched the table.

"Do you remember how Mama wanted us to go to church?"

"What brought that up?"

"There are so many churches here."

"We aren't Catholic."

"Anyway, there are a lot of churches here and I remember once Mama was talking about God to you because you were being naughty and you said, so crossly, 'I hate God.' And Mama said, "Victor, God doesn't care what you think.' And you looked so surprised."

"Because I thought he should. Care I mean."

"Mama said, 'Victor your hate is like the smallest most

infinitesimal drop of spit into the ocean of God's love '."

Victor pushed his chair violently away from the table and stood up to avoid throwing his glass of wine into her face. "How the hell did you manage to drag yourself away from Iowa?"

She took a nibbling last bite of pizza crust, chewed slowly, looked at him. "The lawyer said we should talk but you wouldn't answer your phone. Will you go with me to collect my stuff?"

"No. I'm busy. I'm leading a tour right after lunch."

"Can I go?"

"No."

"Where is it?"

"The Uffizi Gallery and you don't have time. Go to the hotel, collect your luggage, get another taxi, and here's the name of the hotel on the river – the Mediterranean Plaza."

His words were polite, his voice calm and controlled, but inside anger rumbled and burned. She is not going to ruin my life. He wrote out the hotel's name, held out the piece of paper which she took. Pushing herself up from the kitchen table, she wandered into the living room, flopped down on his leather couch. In the kitchen Victor stared at the calendar on the wall. Four days. Can I stand even that?

"I think I'll take a nap here.' Brenda called from the living room. "I'm pooped."

You are poop, he thought. He didn't move, couldn't move, just stood. All around him was his world, his apartment, his things - the safety he had to have whenever he travelled to a new city. But it was experiencing an alien invasion.

She is an alien, this sister, this stranger.

Yet somehow, three hours later, he found himself in a taxi near the airport, waiting for Brenda to come out of the Black and

White Hotel with her luggage. His sister emerged followed by a bell hop. Her bags in the taxi, they drove to the new hotel by the Arno River. She put her hand on his arm when the taxi stopped.

"Let's eat a snack at the hotel. I've got something for you."

"Make it quick."

When they were in the hotel bar – two thin cheese sandwiches, a glass of white wine each - Brenda, face flushed with excitement, pulled out an envelope. "I have a letter from Mama's lawyer. I didn't open it because it's addressed to both of us."

Victor opened the letter and read it aloud. Couched in legalize, the lawyer suggested they agree. "Simple arithmetic should make it clear to you both that it will be costly for you to disagree. In your mother's will, you are named as co-heirs. Victor, you have been gone from the city, and not in residence in the house for many years, while it is your sister Brenda's only domicile. On the other hand, simple arithmetic should help Brenda understand that she is ten years younger than you, Victor, and would hope to outlive you, in which case you will have been denied any recompense from the estate. Please talk this over between yourselves and find a solution. I have also enclosed a letter to Brenda and two checks,. one for each of you Aside from the house, these are all the monies cleared from your mother's estate after funeral, business and taxes have been paid out. In this summary my services have been covered and, except for further discussions with you about the house, I will consider my service to your family concluded. I have added a provision in these letters that if you agree to leave the other half to your sibling, in the event of an untimely death of one or the other of you, I will handle that change of title. If you wish me to do that please sign that statement and send it back to me."

It was a stiff letter, and Victor remembered him as a stiff little man. Brenda barely knew him, only remembered her mama saying he was honest. In the envelope for Brenda was the same letter, and form; each letter had a check enclosed in it for twelve thousand, five hundred dollars – the final settlement. Victor sighed with both disappointment and relief. He'd dreamed of more, but then his mother had been sick for a long time, and Brenda hadn't worked for years. It was enough to pay his rent for a few months; he could eat, maybe even travel. Why not to Venice on the train? Then that idea struck him. Why not take Brenda; somehow convince her to do what he wanted? Really work on her. But he had to get her away from everybody. Brenda looked at her check without saying anything. Finally she lurched up, falling against their small table. "What do I do with this crummy check? It's in American dollars."

"I'll help you at the bank." He stood up, put on his jacket, "But not today. I'll call you."

Brenda's face was glum."You always say that."

"This time I mean it. Let's plan a trip somewhere."

"Where?" Her voice was cross. "I just got here. I haven't even seen my room."

"Go rest. I'll walk home. I just had an idea."

His voice was smooth, a voice she remembered as the one he used when he was about to make trouble. But she watched him go out of the hotel bar, without saying anything. Her suitcases were already in the room, so she took the elevator, an elevator with mirrors so she could look at herself, but didn't, not for long anyway. The room was small but had a big bed, and a window overlooking the river; she let herself fall spread eagled on her back, let all her thoughts dissolve, let herself sleep.

Victor walked briskly along the river, then up through the narrow roads to the Doumo, then turned onto Via Ricasoli. Yes why not take Brenda to Venice? Why not push her into one of the canals? The idea struck him as brilliant. Those small feet of hers - she ought to be easy to get off balance; she probably can't swim. Yes!! I'd have to do it at night. The Venetians were famous for bumping off anyone they didn't like. Rivals or problems for the elites of the city were dumped at night into the dark canal waters.

He walked around the rest of the day massaging the thought, picturing himself pushing her into the water, the look of surprise on her face; nobody around, then back on the train. They had to sign the agreements and send them back right away. And maybe he could woo her check out of her before the trip – another twelve thousand wouldn't hurt. Classic. Perfect. He felt a wave of obscene joy.

CHAPTER FIVE

When Brenda woke up, it was dark outside, and raining. She was cold and hungry. Once on her feet, she looked out the window; people were walking around in the rain.

I have no Euros. What good's a stupid check? I don't know how to cash it in Italy. I can't use my card all the time. What good has it done to come all this way? Just to talk to Victor? He's horrid to me. And he wants to sell the house. She sat on the edge of the bed and cried.

I don't want to lose the house. I wish I were there right now. That's my house, mine and Mama's; she wouldn't want me to sell it. I don't want to sell it. Maybe I could offer to buy Victor's half. I could give him all this money and tell him I'll get a job when I go back home. I'll pay him so much a month. Victor likes living in Europe; he doesn't want to go back to America.

Energized by these thoughts of going home, she stumped around, washing her face, brushing her teeth, dressing – she put fresh nail polish on her fingernails, fiddled with little bottles of stuff in the bathroom. But tears still came – this time for her mama. Oh Mama, I miss you. All the sweet things you gave me. So many treats in that house that you bought me. How can I leave all my dolls, or the salt and pepper collection Daddy started for me? Mama loved to shop for me. She loved me. All those piles and piles of clothes, those pretty rings and bracelets. I can't throw them all away. And it's too much work to decide what to keep.

A sudden passion came over her. I'm hungry. I have to eat to survive all this. Maybe I should buy some wine. She wasn't supposed to drink anymore; she'd promised Mama. But she knew drinking would make her stronger. She tore open her handbag, scrabbled in its depth, found the name of the restaurant the hotel clerk had recommended - the one she'd eaten at before. Pulling on her warmest sweater, she grabbed her coat, went downstairs, marched to the desk. The smooth faced young woman smiled at her and called a taxi.

They're nice here, they help me. She smiled back.

Brenda showed the taxi driver the name of the restaurant on its card: Chaio! In fifteen minutes they were there, the restaurant full of people eating, the familiar smell of meat, and sauces, and wine. She asked for steak and salad again, and then ordered a half carafe of red wine. Soon she was happy - eating, drinking, listening to the owner showering his guest with operatic arias. Once again he came over, smiled, and touched her hair while he sang. Brenda experienced an intense and sudden ecstasy, as brief as his smile, but like nothing she'd ever experienced before. She tried to talk herself down from it: I suppose it's because I like his steak, but maybe he feels good about me. Maybe I'll stay here - in Florence. Victor might relent about his extra room, or he could help me find an apartment. I won't have to use my credit card all the time. I've got some money now – next time I see Victor I'll ask him to cash my check for me.

It was dark when she emerged from the restaurant. The street was deserted and a stench of urine hung in the air; all the gorgeous food odors had vanished. She stood for a moment wondering what to do. Then she remembered the piazza with the taxi stand was nearby, and walked there. Three thin young men in leather jackets passed her in the narrow lane; one muttered something, the others laughed. They're making fun of me. I'm back in the real world. She hired a taxi in the piazza and it was taking her back to the hotel, when she suddenly changed her mind. I'll talk to Victor tonight! She used the last of her Euros to pay the driver in front of her brother's apartment, but had no money for a tip; the driver muttered angrily as he drove away.

Victor answered the buzzer, invited her up, but regretted it immediately. Drunk, two hundred and fifty pounds angry, Brenda was saying things like: "Do you remember Mama died this same day last month? Do you remember? Do you care? It's our anniversary."

She began crashing through the apartment, bashing into furniture, not exactly in a fury, more a total confusion of who she was and what she was doing there. Victor tried to slow her down but she refused to listen. She rattled the door knob of the workroom. "Why don't you open this? Let me see what you're doing."

He was glad he'd locked it. He felt a certain amount of fear – his sister was a large angry woman. "I'm on my way out, Brenda." He spoke softly as he sidled over to the door but she ignored him, began yanking the doorknob of the workroom.

"Why is this room locked? Have you any wine? I'm thirsty."

She raged on and on, sucking him toward her, flattening him -that's how he thought. I should get out. Putting on a suit jacket, he wound a scarf around his neck. She came over, pulled on the scarf, tightening it."Why are you wearing that suit? You're dressed up. Where are you going?"

"Out."

She sat down, eyes red with drink, "Tonight? Why?'"

"To get some fresh air."

"Let's drink wine. I had such a good dinner tonight," she leaned her head back against the couch. "What do you do in that room?" He walked over to stand in front of the locked door, thinking once again: She's a giant sheet of fly paper sucking me into her. Like Mama. Yes she's like Mama. I can't tell her I'm eating in a restaurant; she'll go with me.

"I want to walk with you." But Brenda's eyes were closing. "I used to walk around the house back home. But it's pretty crowded now, the house is."

"Crowded with what?"

But she'd fallen asleep, still sitting up. Victor, stared down at her, then covering her with a blanket, he paused. A brief whiff of sentiment rose within him, a surprising memory of doing that when she was a little girl. But he shook it away as ridiculous; this was no little sister anymore. In minutes, he was down the stairs and outside. Later, when he returned, he saw she'd fallen sideways and was snoring.

In the morning, when she woke up, Brenda thought: I won't cry for Mama in Florence. The house in Cedar Rapid is full of all the shopping treats that she bought me, and that makes me remember everything. But here in Florence I don't seem to have any memories. Maybe that's good. Selling the house won't be easy, somebody, mainly me will have to clean it all out; get rid of everything. The thought of all that work, of all those decisions, made her close her eyes and try to sleep again. Then she remembered. I'm on Victor's couch. She looked around for her brother. Just then, once again dressed in a suit, Victor came into the living room. She sat up, eyes swollen and red.

"Where are you going?"

"I've got work to do. A project."

In fact he was going to the plaza, was going to slip a child away, but first he had to get rid of his sister. He needed the apartment. Stumbling to her feet, still in her wrinkled and dirty sack dress, Brenda yawned, scrubbed her head so that her hair stood up. "Can I come along?

"No. It's a special project."

"Is there coffee?"

"Yes,"

She bruised her way through furniture to the bathroom. When she came out, face shining, hair still uncombed, Victor was in the kitchen making coffee in a small precise coffee maker, the raw noise a proclamation of normalcy. She came over to lean on him."Do you have money?"

"Why?" He didn't look up.

"I'll buy some wine. We'll toast our Mama."

I hate my sister, Victor thought. I hate her. He could feel the walls of his brain slamming open with that feeling, but managed to say nothing. Standing up in the kitchen, in silence, they drank small cups of expresso.

Neither knew that thoughts are things.

A brief wave of self-revelation sometimes came over Victor, but it vanished quickly, as waves do. Victor did not want to think taking nude photos of toddlers was morally wrong, and could harm not only them, but himself. He'd never taken any photos himself, only sold them. But even with the American check in his pocket, he was afraid, because he owed money to unpleasant men who would pursue him if he failed to pay them in the currency of abuse that he'd signed up for. Just as Brenda didn't imagine tossing down loads of wine would release a rage and bitterness that she'd suppressed for years, that eating too much food could create a tension in her that was sometimes unbearable.

She hadn't asked Jesus to protect her from herself.

CHAPTER SIX

Victor, in the plaza, walked up and down the line of nursery school toddlers, eyeing them from a video photographer's perspective. He barely noticed the fog that clung to the ground behind the merry-go-round. He didn't see Carlos because Carlos wasn't there. The teachers were, but the three women were arguing about who would collect their coffees from Estelle's café. They didn't notice any wisps of fog, nor did Estelle, busy serving customers, none of whom glanced at a thin tourist drifting up and down looking at nursery school children. Victor was free to act. He knew what he wanted and quickly settled on one or two little darlings.

Look at 'em - all in a row-giggling and squirming, all waiting for the merry-go-round. I like the little blonde girl. The blond boy's a sweetheart - and the dark haired chubby one. All of them in a row on the bench – like chocolates. Careful. Those teachers are watching, but the younger ones won't know much. Walk slow, real slow. Smile. The blond boy's older. I don't like his face. He might be trouble. The dark-haired one's a real doll.

Victor's Italian was just good enough to woo smiles from most of them. "Hi, there. Waiting for the carousel? Aren't you lucky? Who's your little friend? Hi, what's your name?"

The teachers walked slowly toward him, still arguing. Keep moving. Smile at the women. "Buongiorno, Signoras."

The ABC teachers didn't smile back. They told the children to walk to the carousel, and off they all went in the same giggling single line. Victor stalked away in the opposite direction. Damn women. At least the teachers hadn't paid much attention to him.

Their argument about coffee had escalated into personal attacks. It started with Beatrix who accused Annette, the oldest of the three and manager of the school, of being horrendously critical and over bearing. A shot back at B with accusations of drinking, depression, and sour fascist attitudes. The heavenly visitors hidden in the wisps of fog at the edges of the piazza were horrified.

More work, much more work for them here in this ancient city of stones. They tried to take down a few notes, but they'd been specifically sent to check up on, and thwart, Victor and Brenda, so they were relieved when Christina, or C, stepped in and soothed the two older women. "The children love you both. They listen to you and they obey you. You're wonderful teachers of young children and I'm glad I'm here, learning from you.

The mouths of the older women snapped shut. How could they hurl accusations at each other after such sweet praise? All three then saw a fat woman walking into the piazza. The wind was cold but the sun was out, and she moved through slanted sunlight toward them. The slats of sunshine looked like prison bars to Victor who spotted her and rushed over.

"Oh look," the giant fly paper sister said to her appalled and apprehensive brother, pointing to the toddlers. Despite the sharp wind, he still smelled her just-woke up-in-my clothes odor. "Aren't they adorable?" she said and waved at them. Several children waved back.

Victor stalked out of the piazza, up a narrow street. Nothing will get done today. I'll take her to see the Michelangelo. Let her gaze up at someone bigger than her. Brenda stumbled after him, full of crabby thoughts. Why is he so unfriendly? So rude? Against all her previous ideas of forgetting the past, she remembered it.

He didn't even look at Mama's pictures. I like the one on the beach in California; she's so there in her chair, though her face is in shadow. She's a shadow now. My brother pretends to hate Mama but he doesn't. I wish I could tell him about all my adventures in Florence: I used to tell Mama lots of things before she got sick.

32

An old woman wearing a long green raincoat walked slowly toward them. She moved on big solid legs and wore big sensible shoes. She used a cane like a metronome, so strong and steady was the beat of the cane as it went up and down, that she seemed like a big maritime vessel separating ocean waves, thump, thump, thump. She looked straight ahead, but somehow did not see Victor and Brenda who were forced to step apart as she walked between them.

Victor walked his sister up the Via Ricasoli, took her into the Galleria dell'Accademia, bought her a ticket with his tour guide badge, and left her, without saying a word. She wandered in, found the David standing all by himself in a large room. She walked around him, then around him again, then through all the rooms, and bought a post card of him. Later, at the big scarred front door, Brenda rang the bell until Victor threw the door open, but at once he edged past her, slamming it shut so she couldn't enter. He marched up the street. Brenda followed.

"Where are you going?"

"To hell, want to come along?" he snarled.

It was an interesting thing to say. But Brenda stopped, turned around and went in the opposite direction. She had a delightful time by herself. Discovering gelato ice cream, she ate several neon-colored flavors. She was doubly pleased because after the first few days of chasing Victor without success, and still thinking entirely about herself, she'd finally slept in his apartment where her brother pursued mysterious activities. He wouldn't say what they were, but that only made them more intriguing. The next day she rang his doorbell again and he invited her up.

"You're burning through Mama's money pretty fast."

She'd come for lunch with a bag of sweet buns. He furnished the butter and cheese.

"It's all going on my card."

"Why don't you change your check into Euros?"

She looked blank.

"I'll help you set up a bank account."

A new idea. It sounds easy But what about when I go home? Maybe he's suggesting I should stay in Florence. And what about Mama's house? The lawyer wants to wash his hands of us. Thinking that, she said, "We're supposed to decide what to do about the house."

They were sitting, once again in the kitchen. Victor sat sideways, as though looking for someone else to come in.

" Has it stopped raining?" he asked, and pushing away his plate, jumped up.

"Yes. But the stones are wet. I nearly slipped and fell."

By then Victor was in the living room, shrugging on his raincoat. Outside the air will be pure, Victor thought, the light dim but somehow pure, a strange combination of light and dark that I've never seen anywhere but Florence. "Come on, come on let's go." He made fluttering motions with his hands. Obediently, she rose, and putting on her coat as she went down the stairs, followed him out into the street.

"Goodbye," he suddenly called out and rushed away. She watched him; he was almost running. Just like when I followed him too closely on the way to school. But turning around she saw the front door wasn't shut tight. I wonder, she thought, I wonder if I can get into the apartment. She managed to go up the stairs, but the apartment door was locked.

Toward evening she walked back to Mediterranean Plaza. She no longer minded being left alone. The hotel was so near the Arno River, walking around the neighborhood was easy and she never got lost. The pavements were narrow; people stepped down to avoid each other and back up again to avoid cars. Brenda had watched them, and now could do the same. She was discovering she could learn a lot watching what other people did, a skill she'd never learned in Cedar Rapids, but then she'd never walked there.

She doubted she'd ever speak Italian, but she caught the words for thank you and goodbye; per favore, arrivederci.

She ate delicious meals with wine every night, drank coffees and nibbled buns all day, was working through all the money she'd brought. It didn't seem to matter. Brenda had decided "Mama would want me to have some fun, because she never seemed to have any herself".

Florence was full of shops. The clothes were too small, but she bought a handbag and a decorated sleeping bag. She bought herself jewelry, and a Pinocchio. That purchase disgusted Victor. "How can you be so mediocre? he'd snarled."Pinocchio! That is the most idiotic touristy thing you could buy. Florence is not the land of Pinocchio."

They'd met accidentally in a street near the Duomo Cathedral one afternoon."Where have you been, Victor? I went to your apartment, a couple of times today."

"Working," he said through clenched teeth.

He hadn't been able to make an attempt at the merry-go round and clients in Berlin were angry.

"I like the hotel you found me. They're friendly. But I'm lonesome."

Victor edged away, moving faster and faster, up narrow streets. But she followed. "Where are you going?"

"To the post office. They close in fifteen minutes." Why am I telling her this? He keep moving as fast as possible.

"You're so busy."

"Yes, a tour tomorrow." He hurried to add, "all day".

"Can I walk with you? We can talk."

"It's a long way."

"We can take a taxi."

"I'm not giving you any Euros for taxis."

They reached the next intersection, a broad thoroughfare.

"We have to talk Victor. That's why I came." A scooter ratcheted by, two boys in helmets smirked at them. "And it's nice spending time with my brother. You're my only relative, Victor. The only other person who knows me is our lawyer."

"He's not my lawyer."

"He was Mama's."

"I don't like him."

"You're crabby today."

"I'm always crabby."

"You never used to be."

"Life's a little tough, you know Brenda, in the real world."

"I like Florence. I don't know if I like the David. He reminds me of you."

"Oh shut up." He reached into his pouch and pulled out some Euros. "Here, take a taxi to your hotel. Florence gets confusing after dark. It's easy to get lost."

She opened her mouth to say something, but didn't, and took the money. They trudged single file along another narrow street with only a few shops. Cars rushed by on the thoroughfares, but here were only cobble stones with pools of water from last night's rain. They were following an old man with wide bottom and heavy legs turned outward in the manner their grandfather had called 'the guardsman's walk', which made him appear to be walking in two different directions. Victor, followed by Brenda, stepped into the street and hurried by him, but as Brenda passed, she heard the old man humming, a gentle contented sound. She smiled to herself, stopped in the street and watched her brother walk away without looking back.

"Bye, Victor." She called, "I'm going to the hotel now."

He turned slightly, waved, marched away.

Brenda spent the next two days having a wonderful time. She enjoyed dinners alone at restaurants, always with wine, or lunches of sandwiches or pizza with Victor. Most of her Euros went for food and drink. It was fun also to walk around the city, to watch other people. She booked more rooms at the hotel, decided to walk more at night.

Victor spent those two long, long days thinking of ways he could get rid of his sister. He managed to edit the last German videos for Berlin clients, but only by practically throwing himself in front of his workroom door. She was rabidly curious about him, his life, what he did; he couldn't stand the energy of anyone wanting that much from him, not any more, not after Barry died. He might escape Aids; he wouldn't know for awhile. I'm never going to fall in love again, never give myself so completely to anyone ever again. Barry was the love of my life. After so many false tries, I'd finally found the one man who shared my interests, my taste, himself completely. Love like that will never come again.

Once and while, these thoughts of Barry crept out, like on one somber evening during a heavy rain. Water thundered down on the stone streets and buildings outside. Sitting in his apartment, Victor wondered if he dared photograph a child in Florence. He knew by then what clients liked, but couldn't face the actual kidnapping – the physical struggle to capture a child - if only for an hour. Over and over he made the same intelligent arguments to himself: I need money; my clients in Berlin will take anything I send them; winter's not the best time to be a tourist guide in Italy. Cashing the lawyer's check in Florence could create a problem, could be a way of tracing me. I must keep hustling for money in case I fall ill.

Opening a window to breathe in fresh air, he tried not to think about that possibility.

Brenda cheerfulness, her happy-sappy presence, irritated the hell out of Victor.

CHAPTER SEVEN

One morning the brother and sister met for coffee to arrange Brenda's account. They drank cappuccinos at a café down the street from his apartment. Sitting outside, they talked over the roar of vespas powering through the route between two piazzas.

"How much do you weigh, Brenda?"

"Two hundred pounds." She answered so promptly he was suspicious.

"Are you lying? I thought you weighed more."

"I weighed myself before I left. In case the airplane people asked me."

"You could lose fifty pounds here."

"What do you mean?" She was stuffing a big frosted bun into her mouth.

"I've been thinking about going back to Berlin for a month. There's not much work for me here in the winter. Italy's complicated." He drained his tiny cup of Americano.

"It seems simple."

"You would say that."

"Could I stay in your apartment if you leave?" Her eyes narrowed; he should have paid attention to that but he didn't.

"Sure. If you pay the rent. We'll go to the bank and open an account for you. You can deposit your check. But wait until I get my bank card and change clothes."

In the apartment, Victor disappeared inside his bedroom. As soon as he shut the door, Brenda, waiting in the living room, pushed open the door to the workroom, and disappeared inside. A minute later, she came out holding several photographs which she crammed into her new leather handbag, just as Victor emerged wearing a beige cashmere sweater. They walked down to a small bank two streets away and deposited Brenda's check in his account. He gave her one third of it back in cash. She filled out the forms to open her own account in English, which Victor translated into Italian. But leaving the bank Victor didn't feel better. Didn't congratulate himself on his own cleverness, the possible treachery he could initiate. No, he was angry. At first he didn't know why. He watched her wander along, casually stuffing thousands of Euros between her breasts.

As they approached the piazza, they saw a row of children in front of them. Brenda pointed, "Oh look. There they are again. Do you remember Daddy taking us to the merry-go-round?" She waved at the children; some waved back; the ABC teachers all turned, took in the thin, familiar looking man and his large companion. Annette and Beatrix and Christina didn't know that Carlos had once again come and gone, had walked across a deserted piazza early that morning, opened up the carousel, collected his tools, closed and locked the gates, then disappeared from sight, happy to see no sign of those blasted nursery babies so often waiting in the cold. Good, he'd thought that morning, because that day he again had a job at the Duomo Cathedral. When Christina was sent to inquire about him, no one in the café knew where he was, least of all his wife Estelle. No one there noticed Brenda and Victor, though the heavenly visitors did and were listening to them.

"Mama said you'd just stand and watch. She thought you were afraid. When Daddy threw you on a horse, Mama said you howled so awful he ran up and threw you off again. He spanked you right there in public. He thought you were a pest. Daddy was pretty horrid wasn't he?"

Victor looked at the children, then turned to his giant flypaper sister. He reached into his pouch, pulled out Euros. "Here. Buy yourself something to eat. Go back to your hotel. I'll go right now and buy tickets for Venice. Next Sunday we'll spend the day there. We'll talk about Mama, and the house, and our childhoods. We can read the letters from the lawyer again to see if he told us the exact same thing."

Brenda shoved the money into her new handbag. She was thrilled. "Venice. How wonderful." She walked slowly trying not to get lost. She didn't do what Victor had suggested, instead drifted through strange streets, looking occasionally at a small map the hotel desk clerk had given her that morning. I like it here. I'm just another tourist.

She looked into windows; in one shop she tried on hats and bought a red one which she wore all afternoon. The air was clear and bright. She turned back and found the restaurant where the owner sang opera, ordered another steak and salad for dinner, and sure enough he showered everyone with his enjoyment, but once again came over, touched her hair, smiled. Maybe he's falling in love with me; no, it's only because I like his steak, But what if he is really in love with me? I should stay in Florence. My brother did say he'd let me use his apartment.

Victor didn't hesitate in the piazza, but walked through another big one and into the train station. He bought two tickets for Venice, round trip, an attempt to avoid the seductive idea of shoving Brenda into a canal. He hustled all that day, approached hotels and tourist agencies, found work. He could be charming when he put his mind to it. She mustn't throw me off my game, he thought. The words "She won't bother me, won't bother me" became a kind of chant he could walk around with. He landed two tours: One, 'Houses of Famous English Artists and Writers', he'd led before, another, a new one, was on important sculptures.

But supper alone in his apartment felt drab. Listening to the night rain, he at last recognized his own anger. I do not want to a go back to Berlin, do not want to join the old crowd, or revisit my life with Barry. I do not want to kidnap a child. But I can't afford to live here without work. And I love Florence, a city full of beautiful buildings, beautiful paintings - it's where I belong.

Lying on his cold bed, he began to sob aloud; I'm tired of stupid video projects that seem to cage me in. Where have those ideas come from? Why are they embedded in my mind? Presented as sensible? I hate them.

Brenda was in no hurry to reach her hotel. She went on wandering, stopping every so often for a cappuccino – she'd fallen in love with them, had learned to stand at the bar where they were cheapest, and by late afternoon had drunk three, each one in a different café where she could watch, and smile at, different men. There were so many handsome ones. Doing that helped her get lost; late in the day, she knew she should look for the river. Otherwise there was nothing to see above the horizon; she'd discovered there was no horizon in Florence, only city, with every street, and cathedral looking alike when the evening air turned gray and soft, neither rising nor falling, not gloomy but suggesting a night rain. Her feet in the new brown boots hurt after so many hours in stony winding streets. Above all, the Duomo cathedral teased her; it was sometimes there, sometimes not on the horizon; it seemed to move when she wasn't looking.

That evening, though, she was in the mood to be daring. The narrow pavements no longer reproached her. She knew enough to step into the street as quickly as anyone, noticed for the first time how few smells there were. Perhaps it's the rain or the stone everywhere. In this old city smells are as brief as seconds in time. Ordinary odors are elusive, mysterious, yet noticeable.

She stopped to draw them in: food frying, garbage in front of a door, a passing woman's perfume. She looked for dogs or cats, birds, saw none, but did encounter one beggar: a man standing on a corner playing a violin. The music was sweet, and certain, like water or the sky. She stopped and listened and gave him five Euro.

It was six when she came upon the Arno River, at the Ponte Vecchio. The light rain had stopped. The air by then was dim almost dark. She'd bought nothing except coffee all afternoon.

Avoiding stores with arrogant handsome men guarding them, she went inside a small one where a gentle older man smiled from behind his desk. At first she didn't want to buy anything. She liked the satisfactory weight of all those five and ten and twenty Euros tucked against her body; she had in her purse only fifty and some change; the money was so much like American money she could understand it. She bought a small bottle of champagne. Then she saw a wall of Pinocchios, all staring at her: big ones, small ones, all with big noses, some with big feet. She chose a small music box instead, and a post card with an angel on it, a large woman angel with blonde hair. Walking down the street toward the hotel, Brenda thought: I haven't seen a single teddy bear. I could wander for days here and not find a teddy bear.

She stopped at one more café, bought one last cappuccino. Standing alone at the bar, she was happy. I'm losing weight, becoming healthy, learning new things. I should stay in Florence. Sell the house. We could notify the lawyer. But what will I do with all the things in it?

Hit with a sudden vicious anxiety, she gulped down the cappuccino, rushed out of the café up the street to the hotel, up to her room with its view of the river. She didn't look out, was thinking hard by then. Mama would hate strangers in her house. And it's a mess. Full of stuff. People can barely get in the door, or past the teddy bears on the stairs. Who will clean it up, make decisions about what to throw out, what to keep?

She flopped up onto the bed.

I'd have to do that. Victor wouldn't help. It's not going to be easy to walk away from a house chockablock full of Mama and Daddy's cruddy old things, from Mama's collection of teddy bears. What will I do with them? I could burn them. It was such a horrible thought she lay curled up on the bed and cried a little – a couple of drops maybe.

Victor got up from bed to eat. He opened a can of chicken soup, scrabbled in cupboards for bits of buns that Brenda had brought, found the last dry cheese in the refrigerator. He ate studying his city maps, his books on Florence, but occasionally caught himself wondering what the heck his sister was doing that evening. I could call her. No, she'd come over and bother me with stupid questions. She's so naïve! So clueless. I know more about the world than she does. Maybe I should help her. With the house.

No. He shuddered. I won't go back there. Into his mind came a memory of Brenda as a little girl. When we sat together watching TV, she'd beg me to scratch her back. Please, Victor, pretty please. And I did it. I loved her. She loved me then too. But that was then, and we are different now.

Brenda sat up. Enough of those poor little teddy bears. Florence rejects them; all Florence has is Pinocchio. Hers lay limp and unloved in the store bag. She took it out and looked at it. I can't cuddle a Pinocchio. He's a bad boy. She'd bought a book of the story and read it. There was a shoemaker father though – a kind one. She stood up, combed her hair. What should I eat for supper?
Always a safe question.
I'll go down and eat in the bar. What if I start talking to someone down there and he buys me a drink? A scary thought.
One she was beginning to like.

About eight o'clock Victor took a call from Berlin – from a particularly rude and vicious business man acquaintance. Where was Victor? Had he got something to sell? Why hadn't he sent something interesting? The man's language grew vulgar; his voice, harsh; he sounded drunk. Victor hung up on him.
When he went to bed, late; his notes were complete for both tours. He turned on his music, listened in bed to Mozart, then to jazz. The jazz made him sad, so he turned it off and lay in bed hoping to sleep, trying to sleep, until in the silence, so many memories of the past rose, he got up, turned on the tv and watched a spaghetti western until he fell asleep on the couch. He didn't hear the noisy young people coming up the street below, after the bars had closed until he got up in the night to go back to his bed. Then he heard the terrible racket of the garbage collectors.

CHAPTER EIGHT

That night Brenda was one of the night people. She decided not to eat in the bar or take food up to the hotel room but would walk back to the same cafe she'd found refuge in the night before, when she'd gotten completely lost. She sat at the same small table that she'd sat at before, was crushed against it by her bulk in the same way, but this second night she ordered pasta. She was usually ravenous at night; it was her favorite time to eat, but the night before she'd been so shaken by the hours and hours she'd wandered in the dark city, and then the excitement of the shoemaker's attack on her, that, trembling and nearly in tears, she first tried to think what she should do. She'd ordered only a glass of white wine and some bread. Looking up at a middle-aged woman standing like a queen behind the bar; Brenda had thought that she had a pleasant normal face with glasses - like Mama. She had lurched up, gone over to her; leaned forward to whisper.

"Signora. I'm lost. Where am I?"

Fortunately the woman understood English. "Piazza Della Signoria." She didn't smile, but said. "When you are ready, I call you a taxi."

A taxi of course! Brenda had sat drinking white wine and munching stale bread. Into her mind came the thought: You're only two blocks away from your hotel. You know where you are. Color flushed into her face. I figured it out! I'm not totally stupid. An older man sitting at a table across from her smiled, leaned forward.
"I think you are at Hotel Mediterranean Plaza, Signorina."

Startled she stared at him. He looked like a gentleman - a solid, simply dressed man of about sixty. She felt safe enough to reply. "Yes I've just arrived."

"I work at hotel some time. Carpenter. My friend the shoe maker he see you walking. He think you lost."

She flushed; the shoemaker! "Well I was, but I'm close now aren't I? To the Hotel Mediterranean Plaza?"

"Yes. You want I walk with you there?"

Brenda thought hard; she'd looked over at the woman behind the bar, who was busy, and not all that interested in a fat foreigner. Brenda finished a last sip of dry white wine, which she hadn't liked much, and stood up. "Thank you, Signor." She hesitated, "I wish to go now."

He rose too, gave a toss of his hand; money fell on the table. She did the same thing, not noticing how much. He spoke to the woman at the bar; she gave a slight, neutral smile. They'd walked down the street. It started to rain,-at first a timid drizzle.

"You like my wife; she was big woman too, big, big, strong, happy; she like life. She dead now. Sad, sad to be alone."

Brenda liked this speech, though warning bells began to chime. As they approached the hotel, he'd put his arm around her, and she'd let it stay because it was only half way round her. Then they were in front of the hotel.

"Goodnight," she'd said in her happiest voice. "Thank you so much."

She'd skipped away, or at least tried to look like she could skip. He stood on the sidewalk in front of the hotel. It was raining harder. He'd put up his umbrella, so definitely an old gentleman, but one who liked women.

"My friend, the shoemaker, he say you big woman. Yes wonderful, big woman, so warm in bed."

His face had been sad in the rain. She'd hurried on her small feet into the front entrance of the hotel. Upstairs, she'd fallen on her bed, and tumbling into pajamas, was almost immediately asleep. Now this next night, in the same restaurant as she sat eating pasta, she saw no old gentleman at a nearby table, no middle-aged woman who looked like Mama at the bar, only clusters of men and women getting boozy together at small tables, and a tall bored young man leaning against the bar.

Her pasta had bright green sauce on it and tasted heavy and bland; she pushed it away. I wish I knew the name of this pasta; I don't want to eat it ever again. She stood up and threw down her money, as she had the night before, but this evening the young man rushed over, his face tense. "Please, I give you paper - a bill."

Walking back alone to the hotel, Brenda thought about her brother. Instead of a distant, depressed outcast as seen by their daddy and mama, now she saw how smart he was, how worldly. She remembered his kindness to her as a child. When Daddy raged with drunken bile, Victor had walked her out of the house, even sometimes gathered her up from bed, and taken her out in his car. They'd driven around listening to music, until near 2 or 3 a.m., when they found the house dark, and knew whatever scene that had raged earlier was over and their parents asleep, they would go inside and kiss each other goodnight. She'd almost forgotten that brother and sister tenderness.

After a glass of wine in the hotel bar, she walked up and down the dark narrow streets behind it, thinking one or two unusual deep-type thoughts about her adventure the night before, when she'd met the shoemaker. She thought about trying to find his shop again; Brenda was by then determined to be one of the brave night people. But common sense, which she had a fair amount of, arrived. No, I should put this money away, perhaps tomorrow take it to the bank and deposit it. Why carry it around? Do I want to stay? Maybe. Or maybe I should go home.

She walked around a little longer, visited a few open shops, but that evening, good luck seemed to evaporate. Some gypsies stole her new hat, a big red one, while she was trying on a second blue one. Never mind it doesn't matter, she told herself, but a feeling of dread grew, as deeper darkness came like a sudden blow, as it often does in the month of January. The lack of horizon was pronounced; all that existed was a dark sky above the city and the lighted dome of the Duomo, which dodged and danced, now here, now there, a false prophet. Brenda had begun to hate it. Florence did have lighted shops, some busy avenues, shops and bars along the brightly lit side streets, where the sky could not be seen at all. When had she last seen the fabric of stars? Gone was her sense of pleasure, her new courage, instead came a growing familiar sense of fear. There was no moon.

I should go back to the hotel. I'll hide the money in the room. And I'll ask Jesus for help. I'd almost forgotten Jesus. No wonder I'm having trouble. I should have asked Jesus for help last night. Then the practical idea of finding a taxi came into her mind, and she grew more cheerful. Soon she found one.

The night before, when she'd become lost and wandered deep into unknown, unlighted parts of the city, a feeling of being imprisoned had overcome her; a sense of being truly lost, not just in the old Italian city, but in the deep chambers of its spirit, where anger, contempt, secret spites, and hidden purposes, emerged, as did the knowledge that good or evil couldn't pull the same wagon of hope. Brenda had not really thought that, but felt it - a strong feeling new to her, and confusing. As she'd struggled to find a way out of the dark maze she'd put herself in, she thought: Why am I alone in the dark so many times? What purpose led me here in night time Florence?
Preoccupied with these unusual thoughts, she became even further lost. For the city was without direction at night; she met others who were lost too, and the city didn't care. That was the single most emphatic message of the dark streets in Florence: the city didn't care. So though she was not far from the river, she did not smell it, nor see the lighted pavements beside it. I have such a poor sense of direction, she'd whined to herself. I can't help it if I get lost. And I'm hungry. She was in fact ravenous, the first time she'd felt that all powerful need for food since she'd settled into

the hotel. But the few small badly lit bars and restaurants she passed were full of unfriendly looking strangers so she kept walking, dragging what seemed to her an impossible burden of bulk, and selfhood. Walking down a street she didn't recognize, one with rows of dark warehouses, she'd come across several lighted workshops – one was a shoe repair shop. She'd stopped to look in the window; the wide front door was open to the night air, though the evening was cool. The shoemaker, who'd been working at the back, saw her and rushed to the door. He was a square, plain man, wearing a leather apron; his face and hands were creased by work, but his body and arms looked strong. He grabbed a tube of shoe polish from the display in the window and waved it at her. A man who'd been talking with him slipped by Brenda, without saying a word, or looking at her. Then she found herself in the center of the shop, an overhead light pouring down on her head, while the shoemaker danced about in a state of what appeared to be excitement. Her heart sank.

Suddenly he was on her, thrusting his face into hers, kissing her. She was surprised, stood motionless, all thought stopped. His breath was strong; his body was a temple of sweat, just the sheer rawness of his taste and smell overpowered her. She'd never experienced a man so quickly, so intensely odorous. He'd cried, "Bella, bella".

I don't know his name, she'd thought. I don't even want to know his name. She took steps toward the wide door, open to the cool night air. He rushed back to his work bench, found other things to give her, small humble things: A blue leather coin purse, another jar of boot cream, pencils. She'd begun to back out of the store. She could see, up and down the warehouse lined street, not another light shone.

"Tomorrow," he called with the same frenzied enthusiasm, "come back tomorrow."

"No. I'm leaving tomorrow." She was outside the shop.

"Write to me, write to me," he was calling after her as she walked down the dark street still stunned. What has just happened? How many times did he kiss me, touch me? No one has ever been so demented about me. No one has even touched me for a long time. Victor doesn't, and Mama too sick- she knocked my hands away- and Daddy, dead so long ago, always an angry man. No girlfriend touched me in high school. I liked the girls at school, but they talked a lot to each other; I didn't think fast enough; words didn't flow out of me as they seemed to do with the other girls. And they never asked my opinion about anything.

What does a fat person like you know about life? That had come from a deep, deep voice inside her. It had been a scary moment. She'd read once that people have two brains, one in their head and one in their bowels. Thinking this, a new sudden shocking thought came to her – it was because you were fat. The girls were afraid it was catching. The thought seemed both true and silly. You can't catch fat like a cold. But she liked the idea that she herself had "caught" fat from someone or something wicked. Nothing to do with you old girl.

She'd said the words out loud. Fat is nothing to do with you. Louder and louder she'd marched to the words-nothing to do with you, nothing to do with you. She found the hotel easily that way. Hunger was gone; but out of habit she had stopped at the small grocery near it and bought milk and buns, small slices of cheese. As she'd come out of the grocery, Brenda saw three short men walking side by side toward her. All three had dark hair and wore caps, all had muscular legs; each man, the same rippling muscles along inner thighs. Brenda thought they must all do the same physical work and she wondered what it was. She'd stepped into the street so that they passed by without looking at her. They walked without speaking, in a rhythm that had its own masculine grace.

In her room, she sat at the small desk, ate a quick supper, turned around to see Pinocchio propped up against her pillow, looking at her. She'd been startled. Probably the maid put him there. Carefully she'd picked him up, set him on a nearby chair, sat down on the end of the bed. They'd looked at each other - Brenda, and Pinocchio the shoemaker's son.

But her second night of wandering, when she arrived, not walking with an old gentleman with an umbrella, but in a taxi behind a silent driver, and fumbled in the dark for change to pay him; she went up to her room to find Pinocchio once again propped up on a pillow, staring at her. "You bad boy," she said out loud. But they were becoming old friends. She thought of the photographs she'd taken from Victor's work room. They were on a closet shelf. Should she look at them again? No. Instead she took out most of her Euros and stuffed them into Pinocchio's pants. He looked more stunned than ever.

CHAPTER NINE

A few days later, the brother and sister were staring at each other while eating a small pizza - one with seafood sprinkled over it. Victor did not drink wine, nor pour Brenda any. They gazed at each other across the living room. He'd insisted on eating there. She was wearing a new dress, a big black dress with a red collar but too short. Her fat knees showed. He spoke as kindly as he could manage with teeth clenched.

"You're very dressed up. Did you buy a dress?"

"No. I brought it with me for when I go to church. Will you take me?"

"Churches are all over the place. What have you been doing the last few days?"

"Getting lost, walking around, talking to people; only they all talk Italian around here." She patted the arm of the couch, leaned back, closed her eyes, "This couch is so comfortable. I should sleep here, Victor. We'd save money."

"You would, you mean."

"I could stay longer."

"You are going home."

She sat up, looked at him. "Maybe."

"Let me see your ticket."

"It's at the hotel."

They took a taxi to the hotel. She dug out her travel information from a suitcase and gave it to him. It was an open ticket.

"That's awkward," he said.

"What is?" She was putting on lipstick in the bathroom.

"You'll have to book your flight right away."

"Why? I told you I'm staying a some extra days."

"Because you are going home, you've got things to do.

"Without you? I have to do everything myself?" She gazed at herself in the mirror. "It may be too hard for me, Victor. I'm not that smart. Mama said I wasn't the sharpest knife in the drawer."

His temper jumped sky high, but he kept his voice calm. Walking over to her, he shoved her out of the bathroom. "You've got to work on the house – see the lawyer, talk to realtors, do whatever you decide you need to do."

"Aren't you going to help me? "

"I don't know. I'm still thinking about it."

"Well so am I."

He walked to the door, opened it, then closed it again.

"By the way what did you do with all that money you were carrying around?"

She shrugged on her Mexican serape, a shapeless orange coat that Victor hated.

"Are you wearing that?"

"I'm ready. Are you going with me to the Bobo Gardens?"

"Boboli. No. I have work to do. Where's your money?"

He didn't notice that his voice had gone high up with anxiety, but Brenda did.

"It's okay. I know where it is."

"Where is it?"

"It's safe.

"In the room? That's stupid."I'll put in the bank for you."

"No."

"I don't think you should leave that money in a hotel room. Give it to me until we come back. It'll be safer in my apartment."

"It's safe where it is."

"I may need to borrow some."

She glanced at him, "I've brought some money along."

"I'm not cashing an American check in case I go back to Iowa. Right now I'm broke." He took a book out of his pouch. "Here's the guidebook you asked for. We go on the train to Venice in two days. Tomorrow is Ascension Day and there's a traditional parade. I have a tour to take around the city. The regular guide is marching in the parade. You could watch it."

She flopped down on the bed. In the serape she looked like a mountain. "This hotel's expensive, Victor. It would be cheaper for me to stay with you.. I could pay you something."

"No. I need my workroom."

"And we'd talk more. We have to talk." She was staring at the ceiling. She reached up to touch Pinocchio sitting on the pillow behind her.

Like Mohammed, Victor came to sit down beside the mountain. "Listen Brenda, the fact is I own half the house and I can force you to sell. That could be unpleasant for you."

"I want to talk to you about what happened to me this morning."
"
I don't want to hear about what happened to you this morning."

"It happened while I was eating breakfast. After the Bobo gardens, let's go to church."

"Giardino di Boboli. If you walk down from there you'll be half dead on arrival."

He stood up. Thought: There are no fat people in Renaissance paintings, or if there are they are decently covered with long gowns.

"Church is good for us."

"No it isn't. Besides, I have to research tomorrow's tour."

"You're not going to Berlin?" She rose to follow him out.

"No."

At the door, she glanced at Pinocchio, who stared back. They shared a secret. Ten minutes later, Victor stuffed his sister into a taxi, and was giving the driver money and directions in Italian, which he could now maneuver in, when reason overtook rage. He saw how the taxi driver's eyes had widened at her bulk entering his cab. There was no way she could maintain herself in that old house in Cedar Rapids. She'd never done much housework; she'd lost her job years ago, and had no discernible skills except basic office. Who would hire such an enormous young woman? He decided to go in the taxi with her to the garden, than take it up to the monastery. It was a serene place; he'd found it his first days in Florence.

At the top of the hill Brenda got out; he could see the question "Where are you going?" forming on her lips. He waved, than directed the driver to the monastery above the city. As the taxi drove away, he thought more about what to do. Somehow I have to persuade Brenda to get out of that house, sell it, and share the money. The lawyer said he would help her. Otherwise I'll have to go back to Cedar Rapids, something I swore I'd never do, act the bad cat, make stink and go to court to claim my share. All of which would take money. Would I have to stay in that awful house? No, no, never - the house where my father beat me hard and often, where my so called Mama ran upstairs and cried in her room, where Brenda hid under her bed until the shouts were over? No, not even for huge sums of money, could I ever go back to that house. Should I remind Brenda of that?

His hands clenched and unclenched.

The taxi driver was humming a little tune, which Victor found he liked because the neighborhoods they drove through were appalling - block after block of mediocre apartment buildings, without grace or design, They could be anywhere in Europe; this was Florence too , but he rejected it. Florence was cobblestone streets, a tight warren of stone buildings centuries old, churches, piazzas, museums, elegant shops. He knew this world, and even, a little, the world of Renaissance Italy. He could recreate it for tourists. Soon Victor was humming too. I can make everything work. Maybe I can photograph a child. Hurry her home, take pictures, drop her back in the area where I found her. Or him. Always too young to remember me, or realize what was going on. I can manage it. So they might cry; everyone cries when they're afraid.

Once at the San Miniato al Monte monastery, he stayed outside to look down on the city The view never failed to move him. Florence - he loved the city now. He would talk about it tomorrow. Should he say what was in his heart; or what was in the guidebooks? To Victor, Florence was a city that went deep into the ground; its soul buried layers down, nothing on the surface except polite indifference toward strangers, and absolute loyalty to those others who could be trusted. But an intense buried unrelenting anger toward those who dared offend existed too. Renaissance art revealed that to him, and it seemed that the modern city still breathed those qualities. Did they come first from the stones of the city, or its Roman military origins, the ruthless competitiveness of the Renaissance cities, or the arrogance and ambitions of the Catholic hierarchy?

By then Victor was walking in circles on the broad open pavement in front of the church; ideas were coming to him. Or was it in the people, their blood, in their DNA - a kind of darkness. He shivered with pleasure at the thought.

When he walked through the large monastery graveyard he decided he disliked it - full of big cracked and leaning old gravestones, all with illegible names and dates, an outdoor mausoleum. Barry had been cremated; his ashes scattered by his parents, who refused to speak to Victor. Then sorrow scattered itself through him and he walked back over to the long view of the city. Evening was leaching slowly out of the city and up the slopes toward the monastery. He turned and saw for the first time how wide the front stairs into the church were. Did monks need such a grand staircase? No, it was the Catholic Church, or the city fathers that must have built those. There was pride in wide staircases. He imagined one of those grand Catholic processions: priests and cardinals, solemn in ranks, lush in ornate robes. Or even a wedding of wealthy families uniting daughters and sons. I'll research the stairs, bring a tour here.

Victor barely looked inside the church. He stood at the back; it was a dark church, with several stained glass windows but nothing glorious; a few candles were burning, but it seemed unused; perhaps the townspeople came only on holidays. The Romanesque architecture was unremarkable so what would he say? That was always the challenge. No pope or bishop funded it for long, or for any reason of pride? Victor knew that he would have to spend time investigating the monastery; tourists would ask questions. Tension was building in him. It will be dark soon. I'd better go back down, but I don't want to.

He walked into the gift shop and found a handsome young man in monk attire vacuuming the floor. The monk answered Victor's questions, told Victor that only a dozen Benedictines were resident. They had an active choir and sang every evening at Vespers. He invited Victor to stay.

"I'm not a believer." Victor said.

"You believed enough to have come today."

The monk turned his back and began sorting CD's behind the gift shop counter. Victor bought a CD of the choir singing plainsong. He waited for Vespers, sat at the back of the church until the singing ended.

Walking down the road from the monastery, he felt a deep calm. He'd planned to stop at a pizza restaurant half way down the hill, then call a taxi, but this new calmness would not survive a restaurant, he knew that, and so walked all the way to the Via Ricasoli - miles and miles through dark streets - to his apartment, where he fell into bed, and slept the night through.

CHAPTER TEN

Their special Sunday emerged from box where it had been kept. Brother and sister walked to the station single file, Brenda trailing Victor. The week she'd been in Florence seemed like forever to her brother. There was no improving her mind; the tidbits of history he presented skillfully to tourists as a guide in the city, and which delighted them, made no impression on Brenda. She barely listened. He had to get rid of her, somehow, somewhere. The thought of deep waters, like a vision, haunted him that morning.

"The cobblestones hurt my feet. Mama said I had very delicate feet."

"I don't believe you."

"You're mean, Victor."

"I hope so. Somebody has to wake you up."

Sunday was a gray morning, a light drizzle. Victor shivered, Brenda did not. She'd worn a bulky winter jacket against his advice while he sported a leather one. They both carried small knapsacks - water, chocolate, nuts, a paper or book to read – all necessities for a journey. They'd met at the taxi piazza, the only one Brenda could find, but Victor refused to pay the fare.

Meanwhile in the Piazza del Marco, the three A.B.C. teachers and their giggling toddlers were waiting, yet again. Carlo had once again not shown up at ten o'clock. The January wind was cold, though not strong; the toddlers were warmly dressed, but still, Annette, Beatrix and Christina (A., B., and C.) didn't like the fact that the merry-go-round sat silent. This time it was Annette, the senior teacher, who marched into the café to demand in Italian, in an overloud voice, "When does the giostra open up?" The coffee crowd avoided her eyes. "I have small children out there. When does the operator arrive?"

Estelle, the middle aged woman with solid shoulders, stood behind the bar. "Who knows? she shrugged. "Does anyone? Carlo, he keeps his own hours." She knew he was still upstairs in bed. Smiling, with complete majesty, she thrust a complimentary expresso at the distressed older woman, who took it, then, along with several older men, stood at the bar sipping it. The café was warm, smelled of coffee and buns, was a small luxury she could permit herself as director, as long as she didn't look out and see B and C, faces red with cold, moving up and down the line of seated children.

Heavenly observers were there too. They didn't have to go to Venice to keep track of all their responsibilities.

Soon Victor and Brenda were on the train, a sleek quiet train. To Venice. It was early and January mists still hung in the air. Their car was nearly empty. They sat side by side, uncomfortable to find themselves so close, but unwilling to spread out until the conductor passed through. Once outside Florence, they were in a world of field, low hills, and mist. The train was so quiet they felt they must not talk, until the silence was broken, first by the conductor checking their tickets, then by a small cart pushed by two unhappy looking attendants in uniform, a young man and a young woman, who poured out thimble-sized cups of expresso, and passed them two minuscule chocolate bars. Then, just as the mists evaporated outside in the morning world, their own silences left them. They began to talk, not about the house in Cedar Rapids, but about themselves, as though for the first time they could acknowledge a common heritage. Yes their reunion had begun badly; Brenda had arrived unannounced, demanding a great deal of attention, just as Victor, only recently arrived in Italy himself, struggled both with the loss of his lover, and with the idea of a new and dangerous career.

Victor and Brenda talked about two things: First, how they had spent the day before, then almost magically, they slid into the past, not often a shared past. Victor was ten years older than his sister. But in this conversation, each had a brief sharp introduction to the real person beneath a parent's public face. Each told the other a secret bewildering true event.

Was it the train, its silence and emptiness, carrying them to a new unimaginable destination? Was it the elegant, ever distant landscape, and the mist dissolving into it? Was it the neutrality of every Italian they had met that morning, who refused to offer them the least speck of recognition that they were fellow human beings? Whatever caused this magic, they treated other as valuable, as family.

Victor told his sister about the night their father overheard a conversation he was having on the telephone with his first lover. At first his father didn't know it was a man, but avaricious for gossip, eager to insert himself into his son's life, he had listened with mounting confusion, then rage, as it became clearer the voice on the other end of the home phone belonged to an older man, a teacher at Victor's high school.

In a single moment Victor's father ripped the telephone out of Victor's hand, ripped the phone out of the wall, ripped the shirt off Victor's back. He dragged his son into the back yard, and there, in full view of any neighbor still curious enough to watch, had proceeded to beat Victor nearly senseless."I didn't dare go to school for a week; my face was so bad."

"Where was I that day?" wondered Brenda.

"I don't know. It was late afternoon, after school."

"Maybe I was at Gina's. I used to go there to get away from the shouting. I do remember you stayed in your room a lot."

"I didn't know what to do. If I came out he might beat me up again. Finally I went to Grandpa's. I lived there for the rest of the school year."

"I thought mama sent you to look after him."

Their grandfather, a tall ancient man of mild character, never visited his daughter or grandchildren, but when they stayed with him, they enjoyed pork and beans every night, and all the reading of books, comic books, television, and radio programs they cared to imbibe.

"Grandpa probably saved my life," Victor said, "and he never asked me anything."

Brenda didn't want to know any more about the lover. She still felt a faint sense of shocked surprise that her brother had taken such a difficult path, though she'd begun to understand he had no choice. As the train slowed in small towns and then poured itself smoothly across the Tuscan countryside, she thought, Did I have choice? Maybe more; it's hard to say. Shall I tell him?

She hesitated a long time, their silence bearing down on them until Victor finally asked in a small tight voice. "Are you shocked? "

"No," she said, "I just thought maybe I should tell you something almost as bad."

Silence again, and then Victor said in the same tight voice, "I want you to know I'm glad it happened. I made something out of myself without him. I never spoke to Daddy again. With Grandpa's help I made it through college, won scholarships for graduate school, got myself over to Europe. If he hadn't attacked me I might never have gotten strong enough to get away."

Brenda thought, Maybe what happened to me made me weak not strong. She felt a curl of admiration for Victor that showed in her voice. Most people thought her voice small and weak for such a large woman, but now with Victor she took a deep breath and said in a strong voice, "You were gone when I had my trouble with Mama. Daddy never knew. We didn't dare tell him."

Victor suppressed the desire to rise from his seat and take the empty one across the aisle. A few people were getting on from a town where the train had stopped. He wanted to check the facts, consult his guide, anything to avoid hearing Brenda's story. "What kind of trouble were you in?" He knew his voice was scornful but Brenda was by then determined, and in her new, firm, deeper voice said. "I got pregnant. At thirteen - Mom said he'd kill me."

The train picked up speed. A couple came into the car, sat down behind them. Brenda hesitated. The woman looked heavy and dissatisfied, a look her mama had so often when she saw her daughter. Brenda lowered her voice, "Mama was furious."

"Who was the father?" said Victor, suddenly afraid. Had it been..?

"I never told anyone. I refused to tell her. Of course she thought it was you or Daddy. She had an awful mind. Did you know that Victor about our Mama? What an awful suspicious mind she could have?"

"No, I didn't know. Mama was pretty good to me."

They both looked out the window at water on both sides of the train, smooth, cool blue water. They were travelling across a sea, like Jesus, thought Brenda, and at once felt guilt that she had thought so little of him, of his miracles, his leadership. I'm not good enough to be a disciple, but Jesus had lots of women friends, and she could almost hear the church choir singing, "What a friend we have in Jesus." She didn't dare tell Victor that. He didn't like her talking about God and Jesus. Instead she told him when she got pregnant, how angry and scared Mama was.

"Scared mostly of Daddy, but also of the church people, and the neighbors." She looked at Victor with big brown eyes. "She was all the time screaming at me. 'You foolish girl. How could you be so stupid. Who's the father?'

Victor was listening now, against his will he was remembering again when Brenda was a child, a sweet, timid child with long braids, a thin child.

"I wouldn't tell her." Brenda said, "She asked, and asked

but I wouldn't say.

"It wasn't Daddy was it?" Victor looked stricken.

"No, no, Mama asked me that, or Grandpa, or the neighbor, Mr. Clemens. No, no, no, I said, and vowed I'd never tell."

"Good thing I wasn't there, Victor said, "They would have blamed me." He opened the table in the back of the seat, pulled it down, then put it back up. "Who was it? You can tell me. I probably don't even know who he was." He leaned forward, touched her shoulder, not quite a tender touch, but gentle. Brenda maintained a stubborn silence. She looked out at the smooth, blue - green water; the train made no ripples, not like a boat, and the strip of land the tracks ran on was so narrow, so flat, almost invisible, it seemed to her they were taking part in a miracle.

"So you won't tell me?" Victor said.

"No. I'll never tell anyone. I'll take it to my grave."

"Very dramatic." She pretended not to hear him.

" Does anyone know?" he said after a few minutes.

"Jesus."

"Oh shut up."

They sat in silence until they were rushing forward into the station in Venice. Finally Victor asked in a calmer voice,

"What happened to the child?"

Brenda didn't answer right away. She was deciding whether to lie or not.

"Was it a boy or a girl?"

"A boy."

The train stopped. They were in the station in Venice.

They rose, took their day packs from the shelf above them.

"Are you going to tell me what happened to it?"

"A baby's not an it."

"Are you going to tell me?"

"Maybe."

They walked toward the open doors at the end of the carriage. Four or five passengers were deboarding ahead of them, some with suitcases.

"You can tell me. I'm your brother."

"But are you my friend?" She looked at him when she said that. "There are people who act friendly but aren't your friends."

"Well, well our little philosopher," Victor snapped, and climbed down, but he turned to help his sister. She struggled down, clumsy. He cringed with embarrassment. No one on the train was as fat as Brenda. No one he saw anywhere.

She'd found the toilet on the train impossibly small. Everything is too small for a fat person in Italy, she'd decided. In the Venice station they walked around and found a toilet, with a sign declaring it so, unlike the one in the Florence station which had defeated them. Victor went to buy two tickets to the vaporetto or water bus. Into his mind came again the evil vision of Brenda sinking like a stone into deep water, without a cry, a murmur, an objection, just gone. By then it was a vision that seemed a part of him. When he came back, he told his sister they would travel up the canal to St. Mark's Square. Brenda asked if they could take a gondola, but he said they were too expensive.

As they walked to the water bus station Brenda was charmed by everything she saw. The morning, still early – about ten – was cool and serene, a light mist still lingered; the colored palaces and buildings were as fanciful as those in any fairy story she'd ever read. By noon they were on the water bus, which followed the major canal; they stood at the open end and took in the long rows of enchanted buildings on both sides of the water. Few gondolas were out on the water; few people were walking; the bus itself was only 1/3 full. Not many tourists, Victor thought, mainly Italians, perhaps locals or from other cities. He thought about Brenda's words about friends. He had no friends, not in Italy. He hadn't wanted anyone in his life after Barry died. Florence had gay clubs; he'd seen some attractive men. What was he waiting for? Friendship was friendship; love affairs, another matter. In Berlin he'd had women friends, even one or two married couples he spent evenings with. I must try harder, he thought.

"Why is Pinocchio such a bad boy?" Brenda asked.

"What?"Startled, Victor turned to see she was looking at a large almost ruined palace.

"Pinocchio. Why does he disobey his father so much?"

"Why not?" Victor shrugged. He would not be drawn into conversations about bad boys. "And why are you jabbering on about him?"

"I bought the book. Pinocchio. I told you I read it. But he's so persistent about being bad. Is that particularly Italian?"

Oh God, Victor thought; he refused to answer, but buttoned his jacket and twisted the black wool scarf tighter around his neck. He looked out at the ice cream cone colors of buildings leaning into the blue green water. Venice in the winter seems clean, idyllic. Not like the summer Barry and I were here. The smell of the water is the first thing we noticed. Barry was already ill, but wouldn't admit to it. Stop thinking about him he told himself.

"I didn't feel bad," Brenda said, abrupt as always, "I liked being pregnant. I liked the feeling that making a baby was something I could do that would make me useful."

"Useful." Victor was listening now. "You were fourteen years old."

"In Renaissance Italy, didn't girls marry when they were fourteen?"

Victor was shocked; it was such an intelligent question.

"Where did you learn that?"

"In one of your books - you've got a lot of books on the Renaissance, and about Italy. Like there was one on Venice – how they used to try and convict people secretly and then, at night, throw them into the canals. They were kind of horrible, the Renaissance Italians. Do you think they still do that?"

The waterbus was pulling up at St. Mark's Square and Victor didn't have to answer her. They followed other passengers out across the planks to the pavement, then stood looking around. A determined mist hung over the square. They hesitated to move. Victor thought that Brenda loomed large; others looked at her with curiosity, thinking, he was sure, that woman's an American.

I'll pretend I'm her tour guide.

"Yes that's quite true," he said in as formal a voice he could manage, but she'd already lumbered forward, straight toward the Basilica of St Mark.

"Let's find a café," she said, "Eat something, drink some coffee."

"Then you're going the wrong way," he spoke in his crossest voice, not tour guide at all. "We have to go up one of the side streets." They walked until they found a café. Brenda ordered buns for both of them and a double cappuccino, while Victor ordered black Americano.

"When were you reading my books?" he asked as they sat down at a small wrought iron table. Brenda bulged alarmingly over her wrought iron chair, but the young man behind the bar was smiling at Victor, who'd become aware of him as soon as they'd entered.

"I go in there sometimes when you aren't there. You did give me a key, remember? I've been reading a lot about Italy. But how come your study door is always locked?"

Victor felt his whole self shrunk, focused, alarmed, his thoughts pulling him down into the smallest, meanest voice he could muster. "Don't go in that room!"

"Why not?"

"You don't tell me who fathered your child; I don't tell you what I'm doing in that room."

Brenda stared at him, blinked slowly. "Sometimes your apartment door doesn't lock. Did you know that?"

He didn't reply.

.

CHAPTER ELEVEN

Victor and Brenda's day in Venice wore on. They looked into shops that were open. Victor bought a cap on sale, black, and rather dashing, he thought. Brenda left her scarf at a kiosk where she bought postcards, and they rushed back to retrieve it. They wandered up and down over small bridges along lanes full of smart shops where women tried on sale suits and dresses. Brenda went inside small shops, to find the clothes all too small, and came out flustered and annoyed. Nothing ever fits me. She bought small charms for her one girlfriend, Gina, who had two children and a handsome husband.

They returned to St. Mark's Square. Brenda wandered toward the Basilica which she found strange and intriguing; Victor waited for her some distance away. Stray mist lingered throughout the square, giving it an air of mystery. He secretly thought the exterior hideous and decided he would never be a tour guide in Venice for he dared tell no one that. He'd read John Ruskin's famous book, The Stones of Venice, and appreciated the complexity of the world of medieval Venice, but seeing the building itself remained a shock.

The city itself seemed alien too. He sat on a bench, groping for a word that would suit it —alarming. Why do I think that? Because of the water, the dangers of good and evil that water offered – so smooth, secretive, neutral, the depth of it, the creatures in it, its inhospitality toward man, toward woman – he amended – and let his thoughts circle around the word 'woman'. Even a fat woman could disappear in one of those back channels. If only he knew the city better, had maps, especially of the waterways; the idea seemed an outrageous plan, but the vision wouldn't leave him: Brenda plunging down through water, not even crying out, water all around and above her, clean water, blue, green, or even golden at twilight.

Did he see himself there? Was he standing watching? He couldn't see himself. He had no imagination at the best of times. Every day Barry used to pick out my clothes, tell me what to wear. I miss that, he thought. How sweet, how simple: someone says to you: put this shirt on, those trousers, wear that tie, take a sweater, that cap, no not that tatty old one. Like a parent. His mother had until one day he'd rebelled. Never mind he thought. She's dead, Daddy's dead; soon we all will be. When will I know? Barry didn't tell me when we were here; he was probably already sick when we visited.

Brenda came out of the Basilica. She hadn't like it. "It's full of Jesus dying on the cross," she told her brother. "I don't like them showing Jesus that way. They have places where they baptize people, tall places. You can baptize yourself." Her voice was full of wonder. She thought, with a secret tickle of pleasure, Mama wouldn't approve. Mama would hate it that she was in a Catholic church during a mass. "They were doing a mass."

"Celebrating," Victor corrected her.

"Have you gone to mass?"

"Sometimes."

"Mama would hate that."

"Mama hasn't been in my life much lately."

Brenda's eyes filled with tears, a sudden caving in.

"Sometimes I miss her. She was so sick at the end."

"Let's go eat, "Victor said.

They walked away from the Basilica. The day was advancing, the square filling up with people. People were going into mass, walking through pigeons, feeding them, chatting to each other. The mist had dissolved and the mid-day sky was a high mild gray, tinged with blue; the air was warmer. "One more walk around, then an early supper. We have to catch our train."

"Why do they call it celebrating when they're always crucifying Jesus. The saints don't look that happy either."

"Keep your voice down," Victor hissed. Brenda felt another stab of pleasure; her voice was too loud. A new sin - she wanted to talk about sin. Mama had talked a lot about it and the discussion invariably grew confusing: Major sins, minor sins, everybody behaving sinfully.

"What about babies," she'd asked Mama once.

"Babies are without sin, except Catholic babies; they're born with it."

"Was my baby born without sin?"

Mama's face had darkened; she'd wandered away on her stick legs without answering. Brenda didn't know if the father was Catholic or not. She hadn't known him very well, nor very long. By then Victor had found a restaurant opening for dinner; they were the first to enter. They sat across from each other. Victor ordered wine.

"What do you think about sin?" she asked her brother.

"Do we have to talk about sin, about babies?" His voice was peevish, an old man's.

Brenda looked at him. Her brother was getting old, dried up. She hadn't remembered him that way. She remembered him a boy of twenty, handsome, full of jokes, smiles even, at least for Mama and her. She liked her memory of him better than how he looked across the table, frowning, tight, bitter. Bitter – that was a new word that had crept into her, here in Italy. They ordered – she chose liver, he, sole. Brenda ate bread; he ordered another glass of wine. He spun the empty one.

"Was your child a boy or a girl?"

"I told you, a boy."

"Did you name him?"

She dropped her head, took another slice of bread, didn't meet his eyes. "No."

"Did you see him?"

"No."

Their pasta course came.

"Was he healthy?"

She slammed down her spoon and fork.

"Stop it, Victor," Her usual placid brown eyes were now a stormy near black. "Stop talking about my life. I shouldn't have told you. You are not my friend."

"How do you know that?" Victor took careful bites of pasta. A wave of silliness passed through his chest. A desire to laugh, but he felt in control too, felt larger, much stronger than Brenda. At last he'd found a weakness – this child she'd never claimed. He took sips of red wine.

The main courses came. They ate in silence.

"Let's talk about the house," said Brenda, eyes still angry.

Victor put down his fork, "If you stay in Florence, you'll have to get someone in Iowa to clean it out, and sell it. We'll split the costs and the money. The lawyer, for a fee, will help you."

"Mama hid money all over that house. She hid if from Daddy, and from me. She hid everything that came to her; even Grandpa's money is probably mostly lying around the house. The money in the account that the lawyer sent was Daddy's. If we sell the house, and I am thinking about it, I have to go back and search for what's hidden."

Victor blinked. That put a different face on everything. Perhaps Cedar Rapids in the spring wouldn't be too bad – if he went back alone. "Did you bring the keys?"

She didn't answer, mopped up gravy with bread.

"To the house."

"Yes."

"Where are they?"

"In the hotel room." She didn't meet his eyes. "Why do you want to know?"

Pause. Long pause. Then he managed – "I didn't want anybody getting into the house while you were away."

"I'm not stupid you know."

There are times when people speak more than they should, times when they say too little. Often no one listens. Brenda and Victor talked, but how much did they listen?

More than they had in a long time.

"Perhaps I could help; go back with you."

"Perhaps." Brenda's voice was neutral.

The pleasant young waitress came with the dessert menu and bragged about the timerasu. "My mother made it!"

They ordered one and shared it. Brenda noticed for the first time that they had the same hands, square hands with modest fingers. Briefly sitting in silence, both of them looked around the nearly empty restaurant – a pleasing simple room, almost bare of decoration, but with delicious odors coming from the kitchen. A few more patrons came in. They rose, paid their bill, said goodbye.

"Arrivederci", Brenda called back to the young waitress, who replied, "Buonanotte, Signorina"

Victor strode ahead. At once they were walking in streets full of noisy people, busy crowded, too human streets, and he led them away, into narrower paths; soon they were walking by dark channels of water, Venice a city unlike any Brenda had ever known or dreamed about. She gazed down at water without transparency, dark water without visible bottom.

Victor had taught her swimming, had taken her to the pools, indoors and out, had held her while she butterfly kicked, and had watched from the sidelines while she'd done her first dives. Without Victor she would never have learned to swim. It was a good memory, one Brenda liked. She looked at his back; he was, as usual, striding ahead of her, forgetting how slow she was, or perhaps, she'd thought more than once, pretending he didn't know her. The water in Cedar Rapids, mild blue, domesticated had been swimming pool water, full of screaming children, set in an enormous room with scores of watching parents, brothers and sisters. Their parents had never cared enough to visit the pool. Brenda thought, I will never teach a child to swim.

Then came a new thought, one that pushed the old one away. But why not? She could meet someone somewhere, some day. But not in Florence, not in Venice.

They stopped by a side channel, looked across at the larger one that held the lighted water bus station. In the near dark, Victor felt again the size of Brenda, how large she was, felt her energy sucking him toward her, like the huge fly paper he'd thought her when she'd first arrived. He was powerless to do anything to her, or with her. She robbed him of will. What he'd thought, planned, schemed, none of it would come to pass.

Brenda thought how small, how frail her brother looked. Is it the darkness around us? He was so wise, so sure when I was a child. What's happened to him? Do I feel sorry for him? Yes, she thought, I do. But I will have to turn him in. Go to the police, tell them what he's been doing in that secret room. She touched his arm. "Where are we Victor? Don't we have to hurry? The station – don't we have to go back?"

His eyes were startled in the dim light. "Yes, of course."

They were back on the train to Florence; the lights were bright, the car, this time a first class car, once again nearly empty. They didn't talk, accepted their thimbles full of expresso coffees, their minute chocolate bars, all in silence. If they were thinking at all, they were thinking of the day, reviewing its pleasures, its colors, its dangers.

At Florence, in the station, they parted.

"I have an errand to run," Brenda said.

"It's late."

"I'll see you tomorrow, "

Victor nodded.

She walked away; he stood in front of the train station watching her. The streets were noisy with cars, with the shouts of drinkers. Brenda stopped, came back to touch her brother's arm, "Victor I want you to know something. You were very brave to leave home. I admire you."

He stared. She turned and walked away again, her small, red backpack a postage stamp blot on her large body. Victor pushed himself away from the station wall. As he walked the streets homeward, he experienced a kind of calm; he'd done nothing wrong that day; perhaps had done some good. He edged his key into the street door's stiff lock, found the main floor security gate was open, pulled himself up the steep stairs, three flights, saw his apartment door slightly ajar. Had he neglected to lock it? Once inside he saw someone had been in the apartment. There were signs of hasty going through drawers. He looked in the bedroom. His cuff links were gone, the fifty Euros on the bureau gone, his two sweaters, gone. At the other end of the living room, the locked door of the workroom was broken open. All the videos, blank and finished, were gone. He sat down on the work chair, stunned, stopped breathing for that moment, then began to cough, a harsh whiplash cough. He had nothing left. Nothing.

CHAPTER TWELVE

In the police station the going was slow. With no English in the duty policeman and Brenda without Italian, an hour went by; finally a young woman from the office was called in to take down her complaint that child pornography was going on without their knowing. Promises were made - tomorrow, tomorrow we will call on the gentleman, your brother, you say? And a look, half doubt and half contempt, crossed the duty policeman's face. He was young, handsome, ambitious, and would go the next day, his curiosity aroused. But that night, Brenda made her way home alone, undressed, lay in bed, thought of the blue-green water in Venice, of the pastel colors of the walls of buildings there, and then of the stone streets of Florence, how they gleamed after a rain - so different, so alike; the two cities, yet why she thought that was beyond her. Will I ever comeback? Do I want to?

Victor lay awake too. From outside his window, which looked out on the street, came the sounds of night in Florence: a harsh clatter: shouts of young people walking through the streets, drunk, half drunk, or simply angry -; the bang, crash of garbage collections, and the splashing sound of street washing. Rain came down all night. Why wash the streets when it's raining? Why did so many young, old, angry men urinate in the streets beneath the dim lights? Will the stones remember them? In the morning I'll call friends in Berlin. This is the weekend to do it.

A, alone in her apartment, wrote notes to B and C, thanking them for their efforts and suggesting that ABC school should stop going to the merry-go-round until spring when the weather improved. Two of the children had caught colds sitting outside. She'd enjoyed her coffee in Estelle's café every morning, and had sent Beatrix and Christina to drink coffee there too, before they took the children to the merry-go-round. But Christina was spending far too much time flirting with a young man.

The next day, once again it was a winter morning in Florence, but the light mist that sometimes lingered in the piazza in January was lifting. The two observers were making ready to vanish. They must deliver their report. Florence in January wasn't an easy assignment; the city of stones knew short days, rain, cold winds, sometimes snow, and often dark edged people; like everywhere without the grace of flowers, trees, wild grass and hillside shrines, there seemed little to comfort heavenly observers. Yes, there were churches looming over the old city; there were statues of great fame, paintings of world renown, all the celebrations of religion linked to a city with a long history of fame and glory, but also of warfare, corruption, poverty, and greed. Florence was like every city in the world since the beginning of creation.

The observers knew the city originally was built as a retirement center for soldiers who'd survived the Roman wars. So early that morning, in that large empty piazza, the observers, who had seen so much, could imagine formations of Roman soldiers, assembled to celebrate or mourn one of their own, or even perhaps to be called into a battle urgent enough to take them out of retirement - just as these two observers had been called back from other knowledge to make observations here. They were as indistinguishable as the morning mist, and no one saw them, nor heard them argue. One of the observers was more experienced in the tasks they'd been set, and so suggested a strategy.

"Let's start with the last day, with the good news rather than the bad. Time doesn't mean as much to us as to the souls we've been observing."

"I'd prefer to make a separate report," the younger one said in an indignant voice; disagreements were rare but they could happen. "I'll start with how we were in Victor's apartment when Brenda burst in. Of course we knew she was coming, but nothing developed like we expected. "

"Not bad," said the older and wiser, "but first we'll start with day five, move to day four, then day three… and so forth – there's more of an observable pattern that way."

"That doesn't make sense"

"Don't you like surprise endings?"

"Let me think about it," the younger said petulantly. The older, wiser one pretended not to notice.

Carlos walked across the piazza toward the merry-go-round. It looked small without people around it. Though the sun was shining, the fog was only just lifting, driven by a cold wind that served to remind Florence it was still January. He looked around - no sign of those blasted babies waiting in the cold. Good. He didn't like the responsibility. He unlocked the gate and took out his tools. I'll buy Estelle a bracelet with the money I made last week working at the Duomo, he thought. It pleased him to please her. From the Café Splendid, Estelle, as always, watched her husband and lover walk away. She thought as she so often did: What handsome shoulders he has, what a proud walk!

"Thank you God," she whispered, as she did every morning, "Thank you for giving him to me to love."

After receiving the observer reports, Jesus said to God, "What do you think?"

"Not bad. Some good things are going on down there."

"Victor's and Brenda's souls are awake."

"Barely," said God, "you'll have to keep looking in on them."

"I have hope," Jesus said.

"You always do, but for now there are more new cases that need awakening."

"Let me rest," Jesus said. He was weary.

"No," God said firmly, "there is no rest, not now, not ever."

Back in the piazza, Carlos returned to the Café Splendide, chatted with his wife, decided to open up the merry-go-round. The mist was gone; the sun was out; tourists, mainly Italians on holiday, were appearing. There were sales in the city, that's what drew most of them - to the shops -, but those with children found the carousel welcome. The toddlers were gone. Carlo hated toddlers on his giostra. They were always falling, or getting frightened and screaming; they were too young, but the ABC school had insisted on bringing them at least once a week. Good riddance, he thought and downing his coffee, walked across the piazza, unlocked the gate, and started up the motor. Soon the merry-go-round was moving, wheezing out its elderly somewhat fanciful music. Boys ran over, money in their hands.

On the plane high in the air, Brenda thought about the future. When flying her thoughts were lighter. I'll travel more, Visit more cities - New York – I'd love to see New York. But I need money for that. She took out the postcard with the angel on it. Did I really see you on the hotel breakfast room wall? She kissed it and tucked it away in her new brown leather handbag.

I can empty that house. I'll sell it myself. I'm smart enough. But I'll ask Jesus to help me. He's my action counselor. Victor said he might come over to help, but I know he won't.

She took out the photographs she'd taken from Victor's work room. One was of Victor and his lover. They look happy, she thought. The other was one of Daddy, Mama, Victor and herself, a little blonde imp of a girl. We look like a happy family. What happens to people over the years? What goes wrong? She put the photographs away. I'll make copies and send these back to Victor.

My clothes are already too big after weeks of walking in Florence, plus drinking black coffee. I think my way of life in Iowa was a kind of secret spite against my parents. It's time I gave that up. Thank you, Jesus, for teaching me how to love my life more. She dozed off and fell into a dream that she lived in New York, was married to a chef, and was helping him run a restaurant.

Dreamt too that she had two adorable children and saw her brother once a year.

Victor sat alone in his apartment for a long time after the policemen left. He had nothing to eat – the thieves had taken his food. The police had found nothing, and left with apologies. Who turned me in? How did they know? Victor never once thought of Brenda. He was glad the videos were gone; they were his remaining ties to Berlin and the group of men he'd fallen in with after Barry's death. None of these friends answered his phone calls. Time to make new ones.

Shall I go to Venice again? It was an idea.

Outside the day was warming and it wasn't raining. If I walk down to the travel agencies and tourist bureau, I might find work. I like telling people about Florence. He dressed to go out, filled with love for the city – the only love he had, but that could change. He believed in change now.

He walked to the kitchen, ignored the pile of dirty dishes in the sink, poured himself a glass of wine, sat down to write notes. 'What a long and interesting history Florence has had – with both darkness and light expressed by its people and their doings.' A chiaroscuro city, he thought, with some pride that he knew how to pronounce that elegant word.

He hadn't loved Berlin, nor London, though he and Barry had been happy together there. He saw how thoughts of Barry came with no sadness or anger attached, only gratitude that the older man had taught him so much about the world and how to live wisely in it. Wise -yes – that's how I must be. He threw on a jacket, went walking; everything looked new and fine; he marveled at the churches and the narrow crowded streets.

I'll keep the apartment here as long as I can. It's not wise to go to Iowa. I vowed I wouldn't return. It would be humiliating to go through Mother's crummy possessions looking for ten dollar bills. I have a few good memories of her, why destroy them? No – I'll survive in Europe. Brenda said she'd send me the email address and telephone number of the lawyer. We'll work it out. We're brother and sister aren't we? The only family we have.

Then he was in the plaza with the carousel already turning. There were a only a few older children. He walked to it, climbed up beside a stationary horse, waited for the old Italian to come by for his money.

"Ciao." Victor said and the Italian grunted, " Buongiorno, Signore." Then they were moving. For the first time in his life, Victor was riding a merry-go-round.

Made in the USA
Middletown, DE
22 June 2015